First Dig Two Graves

Steve Higgs

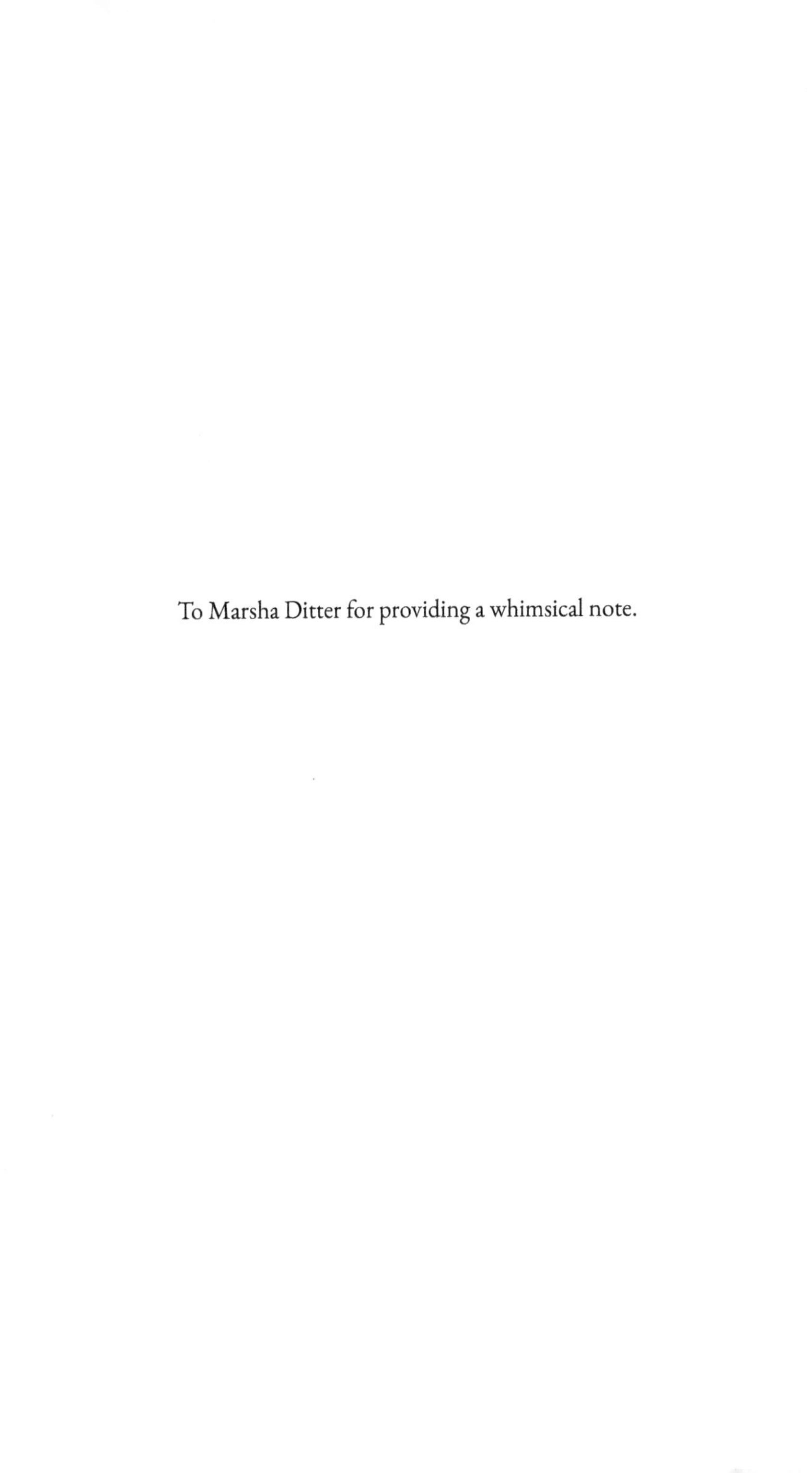

To Marsha Ditter for providing a whimsical note.

Contents

Prologue - Trapped?

They were going to break in soon. The four of them had teamed up, though I believed it was Greg, the largest of them, who was doing most of the damage to the door.

That they had joined forces to get me was bad news of the worst kind.

I heard Laney shout, "Put your back into it!" making it sound as though she believed her partner wasn't trying hard enough.

There was a pause in the thumping as Greg took a break. "I'm injured," he pointed out. "She shot me."

"She shot you?" questioned Spider Williams, his voice unmistakable even through a door. "You don't look shot."

I backed away, looking around and wondering how long I had before they broke through. I needed more time than they were going to give me, that was almost certainly true.

Greg sounded defensive and a little embarrassed when he admitted, "She shot me in the trousers."

"Oh, please," begged Laney, the only woman in the foursome. "The bullet only grazed the skin."

Greg wasn't content to let her belittle his injury claim. "She virtually circumcised me with a bullet, Laney."

I heard Spider and his bodyguard wince loudly.

When Laney spoke again, her tone was a verbal version of rolling her eyes. "Then she's an amazing shot, Greg. Goodness knows how she managed to hit that tiny thing without blowing it clean off, I'll never know. Steroid abuse did you no favours."

Greg growled with impotent rage, unsurprisingly unhappy to have his manhood discussed in public.

"That's the spirit!" Laney encouraged. "Now get that door open!"

Wound up and looking for someone to kill – me, to be precise – Greg released a snort of energy accompanied by a sound much akin to a rhinoceros getting its undercarriage stuck in a beehive. It was followed quickly by something metallic hitting the door, but it wasn't a hard clang which it would have been if he were trying to smash the door down. Instead, this was a more thoughtful whack as something was wedged between the door and frame.

Before my eyes, the door began to move inward. In a storeroom where the cleaners left their carts overnight before restocking them the next morning, I was bereft of weapons, and while there were hiding places, I doubted any would work well enough for the four goons on my tail to be fooled into thinking I'd escaped somehow.

I was running out of time.

You might be questioning where Jermaine and Barbie are while this is going on and why they are not at my side. Were he present right now, Jermaine would open the door and then make the four people trying to hurt me all eat their own feet or something.

The terrible truth is that I have been almost completely shut off from them for what is very nearly twenty-four hours and not just them, but everyone on the ship to whom I might turn to for help. Angelica Howard-Box has my dogs, and she wasn't going to give them back until *I* had ruined my life.

That's right, *I* was the one ruining my life.

A day of hell. A full twenty-four hours of unbridled bedlam had led me to my current point. The ship's security team was under instruction to arrest and detain me on sight. Given that they believed I'd put at least one of their number in hospital and committed what could only be called a crime spree since arriving back on the ship last night, I suspected there were some who might just try to shoot me if they saw me running away.

All in all, this was about as bad a day as I have ever had in my life and now, chased into a cleaner's storeroom, it looked ready to get a whole lot worse. In truth, though, what was going to happen next depended mostly on whether I could hold my nerve.

I ran in here knowing they would follow, and that the door would delay, but not stop their pursuit. They needed to silence me and would stop at nothing to do so. They had little choice.

I backed away some more, the radio I use to communicate with my fellow crewmembers held redundant in my right hand.

With a final grunt of effort, the door I'd shut myself behind less than five minutes ago gave way, the lock bursting inward. The door clanged back against its stops and was caught by Ralph's hand as he stepped into the room. From his jacket, he withdrew a lethal looking baton. That he meant to beat me to death with it did not need to be explained.

"I didn't know who you were," I assured his boss, Spider Williams. "I was sent to your cabin. It wasn't my idea."

"Oh yeah?" Spider sneered. "So why were you trying to get a confession out of me then?"

"Hey, never mind all that," snarled Greg. "She shot me."

This time I got to see Laney roll her eyes. "Will you give it a rest? How about we focus on the millions of dollars she lost us and the fact that we will be lucky to get off this ship without getting arrested, instead of worrying about your tiny scratch?"

"Stop using the word 'tiny'," Greg threatened with a snarl.

Though they were bickering and at odds with which of them was going to torture or kill me first, they continued to stalk across the storeroom toward me. I no longer had the gun, but they didn't know that.

Could I bluff them? I doubted it.

I reached the far wall and had to stop.

Wait, wait, wait. I'm getting way ahead of myself. This probably doesn't even make sense to you if I tell it this way. In fact, you probably want to know how I found myself in this predicament in the first place.

For that, I'm going to have to go all the way back to last night when I arrived back in my suite on board the Aurelia and found my sausage dogs were missing.

Quit and Admit

I was leaning against the breakfast bar, my hands shaking from a combination of rage, adrenalin, and worry. My archnemesis, a woman I went to school with, had conned her way into my suite and had taken my dogs.

I had to dip my head to get rid of the sparkly lights dancing before my eyes.

"She wants you to do what?"

The question came from my butler, Jermaine, and the very fact that he omitted to end the sentence by addressing me as 'madam' was indication enough of the level of shock he felt.

Sucking in some air, I forced myself back to upright. "I have to send an email to Purple Star Cruise Lines resigning from my job, and I have to record a video in which I admit I am a fraud who has conned the Maharaja of Zangrabar into supporting my lavish lifestyle."

"But that's not true!" Jermaine raged.

"I'm not finished." I let him know there was more yet. "Angelica wants me to say that all the tales of me solving crimes are nothing but fabrications. I have to reveal that I lied about everything and apologise to the world, or she will kill Anna and Georgie." I looked across the room at the bottle of Hendricks gin taunting me with its offer of escapism.

'Just have a couple. You'll feel better for it.'

Truthfully, I probably would, but I needed to keep my head clear. Not least because I was already exhausted – it was mid-evening and my day had been hard.

"Madam, we have overcome greater challenges," Jermaine reminded me, wanting to help keep my chin up. "Mrs Howard-Box will not prevail."

Just a few feet away, Lieutenant Kashmir was sitting on my couch where two paramedics were tending to a nasty lump on his head. He'd been minding my dogs for the previous twenty-four hours and due to that fact had been the one who was injured when Angelica snatched them.

Not that I knew for sure she had performed the task herself. I was certain she had people working for her; some of them had to be crew because her presence on board the ship was hidden from me. There was no record of her coming aboard, yet she was here and the phone conversation I'd just endured left no doubt of that fact.

To respond to Jermaine, I said, "I fear this may be just the beginning of things, sweetie. She will not stop at taking my job and publicly embarrassing me. Once I begin to jump through her hoops, she will just keep devising more hoops."

"Then you must refuse to jump through the first one, madam," replied Jermaine instinctively.

I drew in a deep, shuddering breath and wished I had stayed on board the ship when we docked at the British Union Isles. Had I done so ... had I dedicated my efforts to finding Angelica instead of heading ashore with my friends for what I believed would be a day of relaxation, I might not have caught her, but I would not be in this predicament either.

I crossed the room, heading for my desk where I clicked the mouse to bring the computer to life.

Settling into the chair, I said, "If I do not comply, she will act." It made me feel sick to consider what she might do, but I believed she was a long way beyond reason. "I cannot run the risk that she might harm either one of them."

Opening my emails and beginning to type, I considered the chain of events that had brought me to this point. I could trace it all the way back to the previous summer when I caught my husband in a compromising position with my best friend. As it transpired, it was the best thing that could have happened to me and my flight from that situation allowed me to become a different person - a person I liked.

If you are unfamiliar with my tale, I shall, as swiftly as possible, bring you up to date. My name is Patricia Fisher. I am employed as a detective on board a cruise ship where I have found a new home. Circumstance has brought me a benefactor in the form of a young Maharaja, through whom I have what feels like an unlimited bank account, a suite on board a luxury cruise ship, and a large house in England.

Angelica Howard-Box is nothing more than an annoyance from my past. Or, at least, she should be. It was never my intention to make an enemy of her, it just sort of happened. I would happily be indifferent about her and let her get on with her life.

She does not feel the same. Angelica sees my continued success as a personal insult. She is on the Aurelia for the sole purpose of bringing me ruin.

Thwarting her attempts to bring me misery ought to have put her off. Quite the opposite though, it resulted in her taking evermore extreme steps. Snatching my dogs is just the latest of them. That I was going to now focus all my effort on dealing with her was as obvious as it was unavoidable

I typed, my fingers fluttering over the keyboard as I numbly crafted my letter of resignation. Knowing Angelica would see it, I was very careful typing in the email address for the HR manager at the cruise line's HQ.

"Make sure you send it from your original email account, Patricia," Angelica had warned me. "I know you spotted that I had it cloned and made a new one. Did you think I wouldn't be watching for that?" she had asked, her tone sneering and superior.

The call was made over a burner phone that was on the desk in my suite next to the note she left. Her call came with several instructions, not least of which the warning that I was being watched and had to use only the phone she had left for me. My own phone and the crew radio were to remain in my cabin.

I had fooled myself into believing that I was a step ahead of her, yet it appeared the opposite was true. There was no choice I could see but to comply with her demands.

For now.

I would let her believe she was winning – she made it clear that was what she prized more than anything else, yet while she would see me performing whatever mad tasks she dreamed up, what she would not see was my efforts to find her.

She was on board this ship and I was going to find her. I would take back my dogs and watch them take her away in cuffs.

A tear rolled down my cheek as I pressed send, my computer making a small whooshing sound intended to mimic the email leaving at speed. Jermaine placed a hand on my shoulder, and I leaned my head to one side to rest my cheek on it.

Speaking quietly, he said, "I have called the team, madam."

He was referring to the four officers assigned to me from the ship's security team, and to Barbie, Sam, and others, but I shook my head and stood up.

"No. Angelica was very clear in her instructions. I can have no help from anyone."

Jermaine frowned. "Madam, how would she ever know?"

His question drew a sorrowful look from me. "The same way she seems to know where I will be and when to strike – she has people working for her and they are watching me. For all we know she has been able to get to someone close to me." When I saw the question form on Jermaine's face, I was quick to add, "I don't mean you or Barbie, and certainly not Sam. I wouldn't want to think it could be Martin or Deepa or Pippin or Schneider either."

"That doesn't leave many people as suspects, madam," Jermaine pointed out.

He was right, of course. "The point is, by discounting everyone, I played directly into her hands. Angelica has money. Lots of it. Her son is a multi-millionaire footballer, and she had her own money before that. We both know loyalty can be bought."

Jermaine was trying not to criticise my logic, but I knew he wasn't prepared to doubt any of our friends. "Who in your circle could be bought, madam?"

I showed him a glum face. "That's just it. Don't you see? This is how Angelica instantly has the upper hand again. Someone is watching me.

She even bragged about it, and I believe her. It must be someone close to me. The only way I can possibly hope to beat Angelica is to derail her plans, but I cannot do that if she knows my every move. I need the team to help me beat her, and I cannot have access to the team, because someone is betraying me."

It was a classic Catch Twenty-Two.

The burner phone rang with another call from Angelica. Jermaine's expression hardened.

"Perhaps we can cut her off by refusing to answer her calls, madam?"

I shook my head. "I'm being watched, sweetie. I don't know if she would really hurt my dogs, but I must proceed as if she might. If I fail to follow her instructions, and she does something to them, could I ever forgive myself?"

The very thought turned my stomach.

Feeling sick, I picked up the phone. Angelica was speaking before I got it to my ear.

"Well done, Patricia. I can see the email. That wasn't so hard now, was it? You'll feel so much better when you can finally stop lying to everyone about who you are. Honestly, I don't know how you've fooled them all for so long. I look forward to seeing your confession. Record it and send it to me – a link has just been sent to your email. You can access it with your new phone. Make it good, or I will just have you record it again and again until you get it right."

"Why are you doing this, Angelica?" I demanded to know, my voice quiet and submissive – I wanted to scream at her, but I would not risk endangering my dogs further.

She laughed at me, a tinkling sound of genuine amusement echoing in my ear.

"You know why, Patricia. Because you are a fraud. You are a fraud, and you lie, and you go about ruining other people's lives when you have no right. You ruined my son's wedding, you wrecked my house, you ruined the village where I live. Everything you touch becomes tainted by your influence. I liked it better when you were married to that idiot Charlie Fisher and worked as a cleaner. I realise it's too much to ask that you go back to how things were, but let's see how close we can get, eh?"

She hung up, cutting me off without feeling the need to remind me to get on with my next task – she had already done that.

"We need to take him to sickbay," announced one of the paramedics as I put down the phone. He was packing his supplies away and getting to his feet. "The wound looks superficial – I don't think he's in any danger, but he might have a concussion and he needs to be checked by a doctor."

"I feel fine," Lieutenant Kashmir argued. "I just need a couple of painkillers. Mrs Fisher needs help finding the person who has her dogs and I'm the only one who saw my attacker."

I hadn't quizzed him on the subject yet. Partly this was because I felt certain it was Angelica herself, but also because he was receiving medical treatment and it would have been wrong to press him to recall what he knew.

When I crossed the room to get to the couch, a little voice inside my head reminded me that I would normally be sidestepping a sausage dog. That they were strangely absent tore at my heart.

I took both of Kashmir's hands in mine. "You should get yourself properly checked out, Berhouz." I employed his first name and a tender tone. "It is not your fault that you were attacked."

"I should have been more suspicious, Mrs Fisher," he lamented. "This was hardly the first attack to take place in your suite."

He was right about that. I would swiftly run out of fingers if I attempted to tot up the number of fights, shootings, and general privacy invasions that had taken place in my cabin.

Switching subjects quickly so I would not delay his departure, I asked, "What do you remember of the woman who came into the suite. Was she alone?"

He nodded his head but the motion caused him to wince. "Yes, Mrs Fisher," he replied with his eyes closed. "Totally alone. Just like any other cleaner, she was wearing the uniform and had a door pass to get in."

I was about to quiz him on her appearance when he started talking again.

"She was five feet and five inches tall, and roughly a hundred and forty pounds. Her hair was black, but unnaturally so like it had been dyed to remove the grey and I would place the lady in her mid-fifties. I should have been looking at her face. I'm sorry. I was watching a movie and wanted to get back to it, so I opened the door and hurried back to the couch. She hit me from behind without me ever thinking to check her face."

He sounded terrible – filled with regret and the belief the situation I now found myself in was his fault.

"We really should be moving," the paramedic insisted.

I watched them escort Lieutenant Kashmir to the door, Jermaine going with them to open and close it. He was delayed in performing the latter because my friends were arriving. I heard them coming along the passageway outside.

I knew they would want to help. I knew they would try to even if I begged them not to, so with Jermaine distracted and no one looking my way, I grabbed my handbag, stuffed the burner phone into it and went out through Jermaine's adjoining butler's cabin.

Flight From Friends

I waited just inside the exit from Jermaine's cabin until the last of my friends had gone into my suite. Once the door closed, I slipped out, closing his door behind me, and turning right. I was heading for a bank of elevators just fifty yards away. From there I could access the rest of the ship.

I needed time to think ... time to come up with a way to catch Angelica.

First though, it was time to run. The sound of exclamations from inside my suite were faint, but I heard them, nevertheless. It took them only seconds to question where I was, a few more to question if I was just in my bedroom, and then just another one or two to realise I had pulled a vanishing act.

When they burst from my suite and into the passageway again, I had just made it around the corner and out of sight, but I couldn't slow down.

Barbie yelled, "Patty!"

I called back, "I have to do this alone! If she sees me getting help, think about what she might do!"

The sudden sound of feet running in the passageway I had just left announced the imminent arrival of my friends. Barbie would not be among them – she had twisted her left ankle earlier today and needed to keep the weight off it.

With a glance over my shoulder, I checked the escalators. I was standing in front of the elevators and could see the leftmost of the two had left deck nineteen – it was seconds away, but would it get to me before my friends arrived? Behind me was the ship's central leisure area, an opening filled with shops, arcades, cinemas, bars, and more that plunged four decks through the centre of the ship. Once I was among the throng of passengers bustling here and there, I would be almost impossible to find.

Looking to escape the top deck and my friends, I could take the escalator, but dismissed it because they would be able to spot me. The elevator promised a cleaner getaway.

But only if it got to me in time.

The running feet were coming closer, the distance short enough that they could cover it at a full sprint. I cursed myself, knowing that I should have turned left outside Jermaine's cabin. I could have taken the longer, less obvious route and in doing so might have given them the slip.

Now I was going to have to argue and fight with them.

With a ping that made my heart skip, the elevator arrived, and the doors swished open.

I threw myself inside, gripping the left edge of the opening to swing my body around and stab a button. Any button.

"Um, sorry, this is our deck. We're getting off," said an elderly man.

I twisted around to find a couple in their nineties. They were heading for the doors and expecting me to hold them open.

I blurted, "Sorry!" and blocked their exit.

From behind me came a shout, "Mrs Fisher!"

Preventing the old couple from leaving with my arms out on either side, I twisted my head around to look over my shoulder. The call had come from Martin, but he had Deepa, Schneider, and Pippin with him. The four had guessed my likely route.

They were running to stop me, but we could all do the math – they weren't going to get to me before the doors shut. With their imploring eyes begging me to stop, I mouthed the word "Sorry."

Here is what I know about my friends. There is no way they were going to just give up. They would be careful, they would be secretive, but they would put everything into trying to find Angelica and my dogs regardless of what I said. Did I believe one of them could be working with my enemy?

Yes.

No.

Maybe?

Examining each of them one at a time, I easily dismissed them from the list of possible traitors. It couldn't be any of them. But it had to be someone.

Slumping against the doors when the elevator started to move, I gingerly raised my head to meet the eyes of the old couple whose exit I'd barred.

I said, "Sorry," to them too, and I meant it. My apology was not accepted.

"Well!" snapped the elderly lady, glaring at me. "I don't know why those security officers were chasing you, but I hope you get caught. There's a famous sleuth on board, you know."

I bowed my head and mumbled, "Yes. So I've heard." I thumbed the button for deck nineteen and with another apology I stepped out and let the elderly couple have a second attempt at getting to the deck they wanted.

The burner phone rang, and I knew before I thumbed the button to answer it that it would be Angelica questioning what was taking so long. She wanted the ridiculous video and was never one for being patient.

Trying and failing, to keep the venom from my voice, I snapped, "I am doing it, Angelica. Okay? You wanted me separated from my friends and that is what I have done. I couldn't do that and record the lies you want me to tell the world."

"Now, now," she chided me, her tone and attitude superior. She was finally in a position of power and loving it. "Let's not have any more of that, Patricia. I would hate to have to push something out through the porthole in my cabin."

My heart stopped beating.

"Don't!" I begged. "Don't hurt my dogs!"

Angelica's voice thundered in my ear, "Then learn your place! I want your confession in the next five minutes."

Just like before, she hung up. I had to put a hand against a bulkhead and dip my head again.

Why hadn't I tried harder to catch her already? Why had I convinced myself I could disarm her by going ashore with all my friends? Why had I left the dogs exposed?

With trembling hands, I found a recess out of the way in a cross passage between cabins. And there I used the phone to record the words I knew Angelica wanted to hear.

To the Victor ...

"Would you like a little something to eat?" Angelica asked the dachshunds.

Anna and Georgie looked up at the pieces of chicken breast in the lady's hand. She was holding them out of reach, but with the suggestion they were going to get them any moment now. The dogs had no idea what the object in the lady's other hand was, nor did they care.

Not when there was chicken to be had.

Angelica gave the dogs the morsels of chicken and settled back into her chair.

"Good, doggies," she cooed at them, scratching their heads. "Yes. I'm going to drop you off at an animal shelter when we get to Rio" she chuckled. "Good dogs."

The threat about the porthole had come to her in an inspired moment. Jordan's cabin didn't even have a porthole. She'd paid for him to be on the ship, buying an open ticket because she couldn't know how long it would take to destroy Patricia Fisher's life. That it had already taken longer, and cost vastly more than she expected, was a subject of great aggravation.

It was coming to a close now though. She could feel it.

"I should have snatched the two of you earlier," Angelica tossed the dogs another piece of chicken each. They were curled on her bed in a pile of Patricia Fisher's clothing. Was it the familiar smell of their owner that was keeping them so calm?

The larger one – the mother of the smaller one, Angelica knew – had snapped at her in the street before. Of course, that had been due to Patricia passing the dog some kind of silent command, Angelica believed. Today though, they were calm.

She wore Patricia's clothes and her perfume. Had the expensive scent been a gift from the captain, she wondered. She hoped so, for it was hers now. Just like the sapphire necklace around her neck.

Angelica twisted in her seat to face the mirror set next to the tiny cabin's door. Fingering the elegant trinket brought a smile to her face. It was exquisite.

"To the victor the spoils, eh?" she remarked to her reflection.

So much of what she had planned had gone wrong or failed to produce the result she wanted, but her latest tactic would make up for past failings.

There was no chance that Patricia Fisher was going to win this time. Angelica had her dangling on a hook now.

"Just like a worm," she smiled again, liking her analogy.

A message pinged into her phone, a video clip, she saw when she tapped the screen. She was going to enjoy watching Patricia Fisher's downfall.

Opening the message, the video needed a few seconds to load. To the dogs' expectant faces, she said, "Don't worry, girls. You'll never have to see that awful woman again. She'll be locked up or dead soon enough."

Hercules

"What do you mean, it's not good enough?" I asked. "What else do you want me to say?" I hated that she was forcing me to say I was a con artist. I was no such thing, but Angelica wasn't to be reasoned with, so I recorded my lies for her to do with as she wished.

The madwoman had a skilled computer hacker working for her – I suspected he or she was also on board – so I fully expected my 'confession' to go viral and be seen by half the world's population.

Angelica's voice filled my ear – she was doing nothing to hide how much she enjoyed making me dance to her tune.

"Oh, there's nothing wrong with what you have said, Patricia, dear. It's just that I don't like the way you look."

"What?"

"You look wholesome and clean. Trustworthy even. I need that to change. We're going to give you a makeover …"

"A makeover?"

"Yes. And then you can try again." Angelica was all but purring with contentedness. "I want you to pick a salon, I don't care which, and I want you to dye your hair."

I couldn't help the whine that left my mouth. "Angelica."

"No arguments, please. I want your hair to look ridiculous. I'm going to send you a change of clothes and I want makeup too, Patricia. I'll send you a picture of how I want you to look."

"Angelica this is insane."

"NO, IT ISN'T!" The volume of her roar hurt my ear. "No, it isn't, Patricia. It is what you deserve. Say it after me. This is what I deserve."

I kept my mouth shut – it was the only way to keep the rage inside.

"SAY IT!" she screamed into the phone. Expecting it, I had moved the phone away from my head by an inch. "Say it or I'll open the porthole right now, Patricia. Which of these horrible dogs do you like the least?"

"I deserve it!" I yelled into the phone, barely able to get the words out fast enough. "I deserve it. Please, Angelica. Don't hurt my dogs." I was on the verge of tears.

"That's better."

I sagged when she spoke, the rise and fall of adrenalin and horror playing havoc with my body.

"The people in the salons know me, Angelica. What do I tell them? They'll think I've gone nuts."

Her predictable response came back, "I don't care. Tell them you are a fraud and deserve to look like an insane hag for all I care. Just get it done."

My brain was working at a feverish speed, trying to figure out if I could get something done to my hair that would be temporary, but also good enough to convince Angelica.

"Okay. Hair and makeup. I'll get it done and re-record the message. When do I get my dogs back, Angelica?"

"Not so fast. We are just getting started. I have so many more tasks for you."

"Tasks?" I accentuated the 's' at the end of 'tasks'. I did not like the plural nature it suggested.

Angelica purred, "Oh, yes. Are you familiar with the story of Hercules?"

I racked my brain. "I remember watching the Disney movie," I offered. "There were some good songs in it."

A snort that sounded like derision came over the phone.

"You're barely even educated, Patricia," she scorned. I felt a deep frown form, but I held my tongue. "Hercules was set twelve labours as penance for a crime. Like Hercules, you will complete tasks that I set. If you do so successfully, I will give you back your dogs, unharmed and just as you last saw them. If you fail ... well, I'm sure you have already worked out that I am far cleverer than you. You cannot beat me, Patricia. Accept your fate and perform the tasks. You have already completed two ... sort of. When you re-record the video, it will be two, and I'll be generous and call the makeover three."

"You've already taken my job and made it so I won't be able to show my face anywhere. Give me back my dogs and I promise I will vanish forever."

Again, Angelica laughed at me. "Oh, Patricia, don't get ahead of yourself. One thing at a time. And don't try to involve your friends. If I hear that any of them are helping you in any way at all, I will make you regret it."

"I am not involving them, Angelica, it's just me. Look, it's going to take me a little while to get to the salons in the main concourse. I'm all the way down on deck seven," I lied, planning to tell her I rode the elevator all the way down when I escaped my friends if she questioned me.

I never got the chance though because Angelica instantly snapped, "No, you are not, Patricia. You are on deck eighteen. Don't you dare lie to me."

Reeling, I had no response. How did she know where I was? I looked around, peering to port and starboard, forward and aft. There was no one watching me. No one I could see.

Grinding out the words, Angelica said, "I'll not tolerate any more lies, Patricia."

The dial tone replaced her voice, leaving me staring at the bulkhead and shaking from the anger I felt. My heart was beating fast, and I had to force it to slow. Taking some deep breaths, I reined my emotions in.

Angelica was watching me, or had a device in the phone that told her where I was perhaps? I stared at the phone, wondering what, if anything, I could do about that. I hated to admit it, even to myself, but she was far more organised than I would have given her credit for. I had underestimated her repeatedly and it was costing me.

Furthermore, I needed to accept that Angelica had no intention of letting me off the hook; that much was obvious. The only way I was getting Anna and Georgie back was by taking them from her. To do that I had to find her, and I had a few ideas about how I was going to achieve that.

Not only that, her madness was forcing me to think of ways I could combat her plans – ways that were far beyond anything that would usually occur to me.

I could not delay obeying her for long, and I had to assume she had someone following me at a distance. I hadn't seen anyone, but potentially that just meant my shadow was good at it.

My heartrate dropped back to somewhere close to normal and a plan began to form. I was going to get her. I was going to get her good.

I wasn't allowed to contact my friends, but that didn't mean I couldn't make a phone call. Like most people these days, I cannot remember phone numbers for people – they are all in my phone – however, the burner phone was a new model and equipped to perform internet searches.

The business I needed wouldn't be open, but I knew the owner often worked late and then had the office phone redirected to her own mobile. Lifting the burner phone to my ear, I didn't know if I could pull off what I was about to attempt, but if I did, Angelica would never see it coming.

Bubble-gum Pink

In the eighteenth deck salon, one where I had never been before and hoped the ladies wouldn't know me, Marsha the stylist asked, "What can we do for you today, Mrs Fisher?"

I huffed out a sigh, unable to believe I was going to say the sentence in my head.

"I'd like you to dye my hair, please."

Marsha's eyes lit up. "Oooh, what fun." She lifted a few strands of my blonde hair, holding them up on either side. "What were you thinking? I could see you with a soft caramel, or even a bold brunette."

I snorted a sad laugh. "No, Marsha. I'd like to go bubble-gum pink."

She laughed, thinking it was a joke. "Wow! That would be something."

My expression didn't change, and I took out my phone to show her the picture Angelica had sent me. "Can you make me look like this?"

Marsha's eyes were bugging out of her head, the poor woman attempting to guess whether I was serious. She shot a glance at her friend, then met my eyes in the mirror.

"Um, I just need a moment to discuss with my colleague," she remarked before walking away with fast steps.

She stopped what one of her colleagues was doing, Marsha's urgent gesticulations visible when I turned my head even if I couldn't hear what she was saying. The jaw of the woman she was talking to dropped open, her eyes staring wide at me for a moment before she caught herself doing it.

A third member of staff heard what they were saying, even in the hushed tones with which they were whispering and joined them in discussing the crazy lady.

I closed my eyes and thought about the conversation I'd just had with Felicity Philips. She was flying out to join me with her niece, Mindy, in little more than a week. They were joining the ship in Miami and cruising with me to New York where a lavish wedding was due to take place.

Unbeknownst to me until I heard it from Felicity, the bride and groom had discovered a mutual love for Star Wars and had planned a themed event. Everyone on the guest list, which was alleged to include George Lucas, a personal friend of the billionaire groom, was coming in fancy dress. Given what they were prepared to spend, I had to wonder if they might organise a few Tie-Fighters to fly by.

That wasn't what I called Felicity to talk about; she had a number I needed which she willingly gave me even though I didn't explain what I needed it for.

I am blessed with good friends. Some of them, like Felicity, I have known for decades. Some of them I have only grown close to in the recent months, and being shut off from most of them now, I felt discombobulated.

Marsha was coming my way again, three of her colleagues with her, though the huddle had grown to more than twice that size before one of their customers grew impatient and cleared her throat in a loud and meaningful manner.

Hearing them coming my way, I opened my eyes again. I was looking in the mirror and at a slight angle to when my eyes opened, I was looking through the glass windows of the salon and out onto the eighteenth deck concourse.

Unexpectedly, what I saw was a face that looked away the moment we locked eyes.

It took all my control to not react. The tall, lean man of Asian heritage was in his early twenties and trying very hard to look like he wasn't looking. It wasn't my imagination though. I'd caught his eye and now looking through my fringe so he would see my eyes, I caught him again when he chanced a glance my way.

In my head, I said, 'Bingo.'

"Terribly sorry, Mrs Fisher," Marsha began with an apology. "We don't seem to have the supplies to meet your requirements today. We might be able to source them in a few days' time when we reach Rio de Janeiro. Will that be soon enough?" she asked.

"It will give you time to consider if this really is the new look for you," added a colleague whose name escaped me.

I exhaled slowly and deliberately.

"I need to use the restroom," I announced, sliding forward in my salon chair so my toes touched the floor. "You have one in the back, yes? Perhaps one of you can show me where it is?"

Taken by surprise – Marsha had been expecting me to argue or get upset maybe, she floundered.

"Oh, ah, yes. Of course, Mrs Fisher. I'll, um ... I'll show you where it i s."

Certain I was being watched, I needed to create ways to pass messages and tell people the truth. This was the start of my fight back. I might end up with silly hair and a daft costume, but I was going to bring Angelica down if it killed me.

The moment we were out of sight, I grabbed Marsha's arm and spun her around to face me.

"Marsha, I need your help. You have to get a message to my friends, but no one can see you do it." I got the startled look I expected. "You are also going to have to find the supplies you need and dye my hair. It's not something I want you to do, trust me on this. However, I am not being given a choice."

Her mouth opened and closed twice before she said, "Um."

I looked around, spotting a box of tissues and yanking one out. I needed something to write with, but a pen would just rip the delicate tissue paper, so I used an eyebrow pencil – there was a stack of them in boxes on a shelf by my head.

"Here," I folded the tissue and handed it to Marsha. "This needs to go to my cabin, but don't take it until after you have done my hair and makeup and I have left." I figured whoever was following and watching me would do just that and she could slip away without raising suspicion.

"Why?" she wanted to know.

I gave a small shake of my head. "I can't tell you that. You're better off not knowing." She started to unfold the tissue and I reached out to place my hand on her wrist. "You're better off not knowing what that says too."

"Are you in trouble?"

"Generally," I chuckled, laughing at myself because I didn't know what else to do.

"Is it a boy problem? Because I can help with that kind of issue. The trick is to plant rare flowers over the ground where you buried them.

That way, if you pick the right plants, no one is allowed to dig them up."

My right eyebrow climbed my head. Marsha was a little scary. I really wanted to ask how she knew her suggestion worked, but worried I might get an honest answer I wouldn't like.

Instead, I said, "No, it's not boy trouble. Are you sure you're okay to deliver the note?"

Marsha nodded, placing the folded note into a pocket of her apron.

"Of course, Mrs Fisher. Wouldn't you rather I just call for security though?"

"Please, Marsha, whatever you do, do not call security."

Reluctantly, Marsha agreed, and went back to looking at my hair, "Are you really sure about the pink dye?"

I sucked in a deep breath. "Is it something you can undo afterward if I change my mind tomorrow?"

Marsha breathed a sigh of relief. "Yes. I can put a temporary colour through it. I can make it pink today, but it will start to fade as soon as you wash it. It should last about a week depending on how many times you attack it with shampoo."

That was good enough for me and I said so, pleased to be getting on with the third of Angelica's insane demands. How many others did she have on the list? Hercules had twelve tasks. Was I going to face the same number? What was she going to make me do next?

The Team

"We have to do something," argued Barbie.

Lieutenant Commander Martin Baker raised his hands in a show of surrender.

"No one is suggesting otherwise, Barbie. We are all here ready to wade in, but we don't know where Mrs Fisher is, we don't know where Angelica Howard-Box is even after days of scouring the ship looking for her, and the one thing we do know is that Mrs Fisher begged us to stay out of it."

Barbie scrunched up her face, scowling at Martin. "Well, I'm not going to sit here and wait to see what happens."

Jermaine argued, "Actually, Barbie, I think perhaps you should."

Barbie's eyes flared with surprise. "What!"

"You need to stay off that foot," the tall Jamaican pointed out her swollen and bandaged left ankle.

Barbie scowled at him too. "Hideki told me it isn't all that bad."

Jermaine challenged her. "What Dr Nakamura said was that it will heal in a week or so if you respect it and keep the weight off the wound. Anyway, what I mean is you can be our hub. We'll set you up with a radio and a couple of computers."

Barbie's scowl stayed in place. She was used to being on her feet and moving fast when she needed to. Confined to a wheelchair was not her style.

"What are the rest of you going to do?" she asked.

Jermaine looked to Martin who acknowledged that someone had to come up with a plan. Being the senior ranking officer didn't imbue him with any additional intelligence or insight, but ultimately the decision on what course of action to take would fall to him.

Ordering his thoughts, he said, "If we assume that Mrs Fisher is right and there are traitors among the crew currently working with Angelica, then we cannot spread the word to be on the look out for Mrs Fisher. What we must do is assume that the six of us in this room are all loyal to her."

"Of course we are," cried Pippin, aghast that it could even be questioned.

Deepa touched his arm. "Someone has been helping Angelica, and it must be someone close to Mrs Fisher. No one is accusing anyone. Quite the opposite, in fact. However, we must keep this between the six of us. No one outside this room can know what is going on."

"Not even the captain," murmured Martin. Shocked eyes swung his way. "Think about it," he continued, "how will the captain react if he knows Mrs Fisher is in trouble and that Angelica Howard-Box, a woman hidden somewhere on board this ship, has her dogs?"

Barbie nodded her head thoughtfully. "He'll tear the ship apart. Or he'll want to employ every single member of crew to scour the ship."

Jermaine spoke up. "Chances are he is going to find out anyway. Mrs Fisher sent an email resigning from her role as the ship's detective. Someone at Purple Star HQ will contact him asking questions. You can bet on it."

Martin checked his watch. "It will take a while for that to go through the channels and come back. We have time, but we are against the clock."

Schneider snorted a laugh. "When aren't we?"

Barbie circled back to the start of the conversation. "So what are we going to do?"

Makeover

The fourth task pinged into my phone when Marsha was drying my hair. I couldn't decide whether I was best off embracing what was happening to my blonde locks and feel good about the fact that it could be undone, or whether I should just avoid looking in the mirror so I could pretend nothing was happening.

Angelica's latest message changed my perspective – trivia like hair and makeup were no longer things to worry about.

'You're so good at catching criminals, Patricia – at least that's the lie you tell everyone. Let's see how good you are in a live test.'

My stomach clenched and my eyes flitting across the words at lightning speed. What on earth was she going to ask me to do? How crazy was she?

I read the rest of her message. '*The man staying in the Hudson Suite is aging rock star Spider Williams. He is, as I am sure you know, under investigation for murder and has suspected ties to more than one of the crime families you falsely took claim for toppling earlier this year. He has two bodyguards travelling in his company. You are going to find a way into his suite and obtain a confession.*'

I was familiar with the story; it had been on the news for months. Spider Williams was released from custody when the case against him collapsed. Like a bad legal thriller novel - the key witness up and got himself killed.

Without the star witness, the case fell apart, though I don't think anyone really doubted Spider was guilty.

I had no idea he was staying in the Hudson Suite or whether Angelica was lying about it to get me to break in. Reading her instructions, my heart was thumping in my chest, and I guess my expression reflected how I felt because Marsha turned off the hairdryer.

"Everything all right, Mrs Fisher?"

I wasn't sure how to answer.

My instant reaction was that there was no way I could possibly even attempt such a thing. Then, like a gong sounding in my head, a picture of Anna and Georgie formed, and I knew I had to try. My doubt was replaced by the acceptance that I had done crazier things in my time.

Nevertheless, I begged a few moments grace from Marsha – I needed to reply to the text message – and carefully wrote, '*What happens if he refuses to confess, Angelica?*'

Her response was immediate, '*I thought you were a world-famous sleuth, Patricia? That is the lie you have been telling. He is suspected of being a criminal, go and get the proof. I'll give you one hour, or you can quit now, and I will do as I wish with your dogs.*'

My fingers could not move fast enough. '*No, Angelica! Please don't hurt my dogs. I will do as you ask.*'

Ten minutes later, Marsha announced that my hair and makeup were done. She did so in a tone that contained an easy to hear subtext – I looked like a crazy person. Stilling my facial muscles so my jaw wouldn't drop open and I wouldn't choke on my teeth, I forced myself to look at my reflection in the mirror.

It was every bit as bad as I expected. Barbie might have gotten away with it, but on a woman in her fifties it just looked ridiculous. My hair style was largely unchanged – I wear it below my shoulders where the length gains a natural curl, but often pull it into a ponytail because it is easier to manage, and I must often face that sea breeze I mentioned. Today the big difference was the bright pink tone.

The colour of my hair was bad enough – it warranted mockery, but the makeup ... well, the makeup finished me off. Marsha had applied a base layer and added mascara and eyeliner and that was all fine. What wasn't fine was the drawn-on cat's whiskers and little black tip on my nose.

People were going to stare.

A knock at the open door of the glass-fronted salon instinctively drew my eyes to see who was there just as Marsha spun around to face them.

"Hello," said a young man in a fine suit. "I'm from Carson's outfitters on the sixteenth deck. I have a package for a Mrs Fisher?" He said it as a question, the young man sent on a task he didn't fully understand and sounding like he believed it might be a practical joke.

I huffed and held up my right hand. I had been into Carson's; it catered for the younger generation and had a section in the back with bedroom apparel and such.

"That's me," I replied, squinting suspiciously at the box he held. "What is it?"

Whatever it was had been placed into an elegant box and tied up with a bow. There was a card poking out from beneath the ribbon.

The young man glanced down at the box he held, his cheeks colouring when he looked back up.

"I'm afraid I don't know, madam. I was instructed to deliver it." Given the crimson colour his face had become, I doubted very much he was unaware of the package's contents.

I motioned for him to hand it over and placed it in the salon chair I had just vacated. The note, when I turned it over, was handwritten with a short message.

'Put these on. This will complete your new look – A.'

Perfect. She told me I needed a makeover and that she was sending me a change of clothes. When she provided a picture to show what look she was going for, I had no idea she meant I was going to look exactly like it.

With yet another sigh, I lifted the lid. No one was saying anything, and ladies in the salon were all trying to pretend they were not looking with avid interest to see what was in the box, but I could feel their eyes on me.

The next task on my list was to break into a suspected murderer's suite and I had to do it dressed as a pink anime kitten. The outfit was one befitting a young lady from an adult film. In the box were thigh-high, grey, hold-up stockings. A matching grey miniskirt with a ruff beneath and a pink latex top that was designed to squeeze my waist to its smallest possible size and shove my boobs under my chin. There were matching pink kitten ears to go on my head.

Holding the pink top aloft on the tips on my index fingers, I shot a raised eyebrow at the young man. He turned scarlet, his embarrassment silently confessing he knew precisely what was in the box. It explained his desire to linger now that the box was delivered.

Marsha gripped his arm and spun him around, pushing him from the salon with an unspoken suggestion that failing to comply might result in him getting a boot in his backside.

"Is there somewhere I can change?" I asked with another sigh.

Marsha couldn't believe her ears.

"You're planning to put that on now?"

I nodded. I was angry, but caught myself wallowing in the misery that was my day and realised I wasn't thinking clearly. I could turn the outfit to my advantage. There were seeds I had already sown and one of them was going to let me bring Angelica down.

Hopefully.

"Can I use the back room again, please?"

Marsha led me through to their storeroom/restroom and left me there to change my clothes. I guess I knew outfits like this existed and it wasn't so much that it was revealing, because it was, though not in a way that suggested it was bedroom wear only. It was more that it would look okay on a much younger woman in much better shape who was attending an event where other people might be dressed the same.

Like a Comic Con or a movie premier perhaps. I looked like a woman in denial of her age who had just raided her teenage daughter's wardrobe. I looked absurd, but it could have been worse.

That I had to pay Marsha for the damage she'd done to my hair was another insult, but I was sure to tip her generously.

Just before I left, I whispered, "You still have the note, yes?"

She nodded, biting her bottom lip with one canine in a manner that suggested she wanted to ask a question. Or possibly lots of questions.

"Are you sure you're not having boy trouble?" she asked. "It sure looks like you are. I had a boyfriend once who used to make all kinds of crazy demands of me. It was fun for a while, but I had to end that one fast when he asked me to ...”

I cut her off quickly. “Trust me, Marsha, you are better off not knowing.” I left her with that as a parting comment and set off in the direction of the Hudson Suite.

Boy Trouble

The ship had set sail with the setting sun, cruising toward the giant glowing orb as it dipped toward the horizon and vanished from sight. It had been dark outside for some time but though it was late autumn, the air was warm.

I was outside the ship because at night there are few who choose to venture outside. Not because it is in any way dangerous, but because all the things to do are inside, and the ladies, who have spent time making their hair nice, do not want it whipped into a bird's nest by the sea breeze.

Making my way up the structure of the ship by using external staircases, I found myself back at the top deck. The entrance to the Hudson Suite was on the opposite side of the ship to mine and sat amidships where the Windsor Suite in which I reside is closest to the prow.

I was not familiar with the internal layout of the suite I was looking to infiltrate, but from visiting several others during my months on board, I knew to expect a small lobby area leading to an open plan living space from which at least two bedrooms and a bathroom would branch.

Re-entering the ship, I shivered when the air-conditioning hit me and watched the skin on my arms grow goose pimples.

The Hudson Suite was just to my left, about thirty yards away, and when I peered around the corner and along the passageway, I could see the form of a bodyguard standing outside the door. He felt my eyes on him, but I had ducked back out of sight before he looked my way.

One bodyguard was better than two from my perspective, but since I had no idea what I was going to do to get rid of him, it made little difference. If ever there was a time to acknowledge the value of my friends, it was now.

If Barbie were by my side, she could undo a button on her top and saunter casually up to the bodyguard, entrap him with a few sultry words, and lead him around the corner with a whispered promise. Jermaine would be waiting in the shadows, and the guard would be unconscious before he had any idea what was happening.

Or I could just deploy Jermaine to start with. My ninja butler would disarm and disable the man with a single blow. Or any one of my security team could step in to remove the man from his post. It would require some subterfuge, but they would succeed.

Cut off from them, it was just me, and none of those tactics would work. I had to try something though. Violence wasn't going to work – I'm a small woman in her fifties for goodness sake. Tackling bodyguards is not in my skillset. That didn't leave me with much.

I'm not unattractive though. Alistair stands as testament to that. With little alternative but to give it a go, I pushed up onto my tiptoes as if I were wearing heels – at the very least it would elongate my legs – and set off.

I was walking sexily. That's what I told myself. My boobs were already shoved up by the daft pink, latex top to resemble two balloons stretching for the sky, so with one hand up to tousle my hair and a little extra emphasis on the movement of my hips ...

I fell over.

I was ten feet from the bodyguard. He had glanced my way twice, but without interest on either occasion. Seeing me fall and hearing the unwelcome squeal of alarm I emitted on my way to the deck, he left his post to check on me.

"Hey, lady, are you okay?"

I was scrambling to get up, wondering if I could pretend my ankle was injured and if I could then utilise that to get him to help me into Spider's suite. Playing on his question, I let out a small cry of pain

"Ooooh, ow, I think I sprained my ankle." In my head I was going to hobble, complain it was too painful to walk on, and convince him that

I needed ice for it. He would see me as harmless and help me to a chair inside the Hudson Suite.

I just needed to pull off the fake injury, so with another yelp of pain, I tried to get up. What I didn't realise was that the bodyguard had just stooped to crouch over me.

The back of my skull connected under his jaw with enough force to make me see stars.

I swore, wincing from the pain and automatically ducking my head again. My eyes were closed, but they opened soon enough when the bodyguard landed at my feet.

He was out cold.

The dancing stars faded as I knelt by his side to check his pulse. A steady thump, thump, thump thrummed under my fingers to reassure me I hadn't somehow killed him.

I poked him in the face with my index finger. I tried it again, this time employing enough force to rock his head to the side and said, "Hey."

No response.

It wasn't the opening I expected, but it was all I could have hoped for and more. Now all I had to do was get him out of sight. I doubted leaving an unconscious man lying around would go unnoticed for long.

Here's the thing though, if you've never tried to move an unconscious person before, it's a lot harder than you might imagine.

First, I used his arms, gripping a wrist with each of my hands. My idea was to drag him around the corner where there was a dark alcove into which I might stash him. He didn't budge an inch. So I tried his legs. It meant I would have to spin him around once I got him moving, however the moment I hauled his legs into the air, trapping his ankles under my armpits in the belief that limiting the amount of him in touch with the deck would reduce friction, I knew I wasn't going to be able to move him.

His legs weighed a ton. They had to weigh as much as me. They say muscle weighs more than fat, well this guy was muscular. And he was tall. I dropped his legs again and bent over double. I'd been going for about eight seconds, and I was already out of breath.

Gasping a lungful of air, I thought about what I could do next – could I just leave him? – he was going to come around sooner or later.

I don't know if I would have come up with a solution to my problem and never got the chance to find out – with heart-stopping horror, my ears picked up the sound of someone coming.

"I knew it!" said Marsha, coming into sight around the corner. "I knew it had to be boy trouble."

My brain had been hastily trying to come up with a reason why a middle-aged woman dressed as a sexy cat from a teenage boy's fantasy was messing with an unconscious man rather than trying to administer first aid. I gave up on that now because I saw an opportunity.

"Marsha, thank goodness," I gasped in relief. "Did you follow me?"

"You're damn skippy I did." She didn't take her eyes off the bodyguard, and she wasn't alone. Two of the other ladies from the salon were with her.

"Respect the ladies," Marsha commanded the bodyguard's unconscious form. Then, to add emphasis, she kicked him. She kicked him somewhere boys do not like to be kicked and I suddenly found myself feeling glad he was unconscious.

"He's your boyfriend?" asked one of the other girls from the salon. Her tone was filled with doubt.

Before I could reply, Marsha turned to face her colleague, her expression ripe with disdain.

"Cheryl you are about as dumb as a box of rocks. He ain't no boyfriend. Does he look like boyfriend material to you? This lady has herself a little holiday romance going on and it went sour. We all know how these things go." Her comment got murmurs of agreement from both her friends. "It all starts out hot and heavy, but then the man gets all kinds of demanding." She wafted a hand in my direction, "Do you think this fine English woman picked this outfit for herself? No! She was trying to please this sleazy, two-bit, hoodlum-looking hustler here." She kicked him again and I questioned what it was in Marsha's recent history that left her with so much anger to vent at men.

Cheryl offered me a smile. "You want to get back into your cabin, Honey? Does he have the key?"

Just like that my brain came up to speed and I crouched to go through his pockets.

"Yeah! He took it earlier and he wouldn't give it back until I dressed up for him."

Marsha was patting down his other side and found the key first. Not that it was my key, of course. It was the key to the Hudson Suite, otherwise known as Spider Williams' suite, and I was going to use it to let myself in.

"Here you go, Sugar. You just be on your way and don't worry about this one," she folded his right arm over his chest, and then reached across to do the same with the left. The worrying observation was that not only had she done this before, but had done it so often her moves looked practiced.

"What are you going to do with him?" I asked.

Marsha moved to get his shoulders, grunting from the effort as she gripped his jacket and hauled his top half from the deck. Cheryl and the third lady got a leg each, lifting them around the meaty part of his thighs.

"Don't you worry none about that, Honey," Marsha replied. "We're not going to hurt him. That would be criminal."

"Yeah," agreed Cheryl. "We're just going to re-educate him a little."

I had no idea what that meant and decided that not only did I not wish to find out, but also that I didn't have the time to get into it. I had the entry card to the Hudson Suite in my hand and Angelica's ticking clock in my head.

The girls from the salon strained a little from the effort of carrying the bodyguard's unconscious form, but they tottered down the passageway and out of sight around the corner where I heard one of them press the elevator call button.

Sucking in a deep breath to still my raging heartrate, I swiped the key card against the lock and pushed open the door to the Hudson Suite.

As you might imagine, that was where my evening took a turn for the worst.

Unexpectedly Expected

I might have dealt with the bodyguard outside the door, but that had no impact on the one positioned just inside.

He was waiting just inside the living area of the suite, lounging in a chair with a mean look on his face and baton resting across his thighs. Both hands were gripping the baton.

I had frozen upon seeing him, my heartrate skyrocketing yet again. What was I supposed to do now? If I turned and ran, not only would he almost certainly prove to be faster than me, running away would ruin any chance I had to deliver that which Angelica demanded.

I needed a confession from Spider Williams. A confession to murder no less. I didn't even know if he was guilty, although the papers had already condemned him. Impossible task that it almost certainly was,

I still had to get by the second goon if I was to even get to talk to the accused former music star.

"You're early," said the bodyguard, rolling the baton absentmindedly across his thighs and back again.

I closed my mouth – it was hanging open. I was early? Like I was expected?

His eyes roved south, stopping near my waist, but he wasn't looking where I thought.

"Nice outfit though." He nodded his head. "Very different. The bruised knuckles are a nice effect too."

I glanced down at my right hand. Only a few hours ago, I had punched a man in the face. It hurt like hell at the time, but I hadn't really thought about it since. I don't make a habit of hitting people, quite the opposite, in fact. I do not recall ever punching anyone before, but the man in question had deserved it.

"I guess one of your clients refused to behave," the bodyguard continued. "I like that you are already in character. Normally they want to get changed when they get here."

The bodyguard leered at me, his eyes locked firmly on my chest in a way that made me feel increasingly uncomfortable. I folded my arms across my body, limiting the amount of flesh on display.

"Oh, come on," the bodyguard complained, getting to his feet. "You shake them for a living, doll. What's the big deal?"

I backed up a pace, but I was standing just inside the lobby with the door to the suite wide open behind me. My backside touched against the door, making me jump. I jerked my head around to confirm it was just the door and when I looked back into the suite, the bodyguard was no longer there.

From deeper inside the suite, I heard him call out, "Hey, Spider, your dominatrix is here. She's … she's different to what you usually get, but she looks to be in a bad mood."

Dominatrix?

With a gulp, I realised what I had walked into. What the heck was I supposed to do now? I certainly wasn't about to do anything weird just to meet Angelica's evil demands.

A picture of my dogs flashed through my mind again. They looked fine, but they were in a strange room and if she chose to hurt them, there was nothing I could do about it.

I could be a dominatrix, couldn't I? What did a dominatrix do? In my head, I was going to have to smack someone with a paddle or something equally revolting, but I wouldn't have to take my clothes off or … touch anything. Swallowing, both physically and metaphorically as I shoved my pride down where I could no longer hear its voice, I strode into the suite.

The bodyguard continued to leer at me, but I couldn't see or hear anyone else which I took to mean that it was just him and Spider Williams in the suite. I had faced worse odds.

"He's waiting for you," the bodyguard grinned like the letch he was and double pumped his eyebrows meaningfully. "Maybe when you are done in there, you can make a little extra on the side with me?"

My natural inclination was to act horrified, but to do so would blow my cover. Instead, I reached out to caress his face – my plan being to say something saucy or suggestive. However, I remembered what my role was supposed to be and shoved him backward.

"I didn't give you permission to speak, worm."

He stumbled back a pace, his eyes dilating. How far could I push it? Did I slap his face for good measure? Unsure I could pull it off, I poked him in the chest instead.

"If you want what you deserve, you will obey my commands." His lips moved, a comment forming. "I didn't give you permission to speak!" I roared. "Cast your eyes down." The man, twice as big as me and probably three times stronger, did exactly as I ordered, lowering his gaze until he was staring at the carpet. "That's better. Now, I am going to work on the other worm. You will be silent until I am finished. Is that clear?" He kept his head and eyes cast downward. "You may speak."

"Yes, mistress," he whispered.

I left him there and made my way to the suite's main bedroom. It was easy to know which one I needed, there was a light shining out from under the door. Amazed at how far I had gotten already, I was beginning to like the dominatrix persona. It was kinda fun and I got to boss around men and call them names.

Not that I wanted to take it up as a career option, but I could see how some women might get a kick out of it. Marsha for sure would enjoy herself.

With that in my head, I was totally unprepared for what I found when I walked through the bedroom door. My idle musings were instantly reversed, and I swore I would never again give life as a dominatrix a second thought.

The Path of the Righteous

"What shall we have her do next, doggies?" Angelica cooed at the dachshunds. "Assuming she somehow survives her current task and isn't either killed by Spider Williams or locked up by the ship's security team for going mental."

Angelica scratched their ears, one after the other, and rubbed under their chins. She'd never been one for dogs and had never thought to own one, even when her children were young and suggested it.

Now though, having spent a little time with Anna and Georgie, she could kind of see why someone might wish to spend time in the company of one. Maybe, if things went to plan and Patricia's inevitable and long overdue fall from grace resulted in her death, she would choose to keep the dogs.

Oh, there was still the challenge of getting off the ship to overcome, but getting on had been easy enough once she'd greased some palms – what a horrible term, Angelica's top lip curled in disgust.

They were nearing Rio de Janeiro and were due to dock in a little under forty-eight hours. There was little chance they could find her – Angelica knew that was what they wanted to do. Not just Patricia, but her friends and the captain too.

Their attempts to scour the ship and the cabin to cabin search they conducted brought a few nervous moments and a need to relocate into Jordan's cabin. However, ultimately, she found their failure amusing. All that effort and they couldn't track down one woman on a cruise ship.

Angelica knew why, of course. The reason for her success was as plain as day to her way of thinking: her cause was just. Someone had to stop Patricia Fisher. It was as if God himself had selected her for the task and she was going to see it through to the righteous finish.

It didn't matter too much whether Patricia Fisher found herself locked up or dead – either one would achieve the same aim, and Angelica struggled to decide which she wanted most. Dead was definitive. With Patricia out of the way permanently, Angelica could return to England and her home village to find it once again a site of tranquillity and peace.

However, if Patricia went to jail, as surely befitted the nature of her crimes, Angelica would get to visit. It wasn't so much that she wanted to gloat – Angelica would never admit to such a desire, but truly that was precisely what she wanted to do. Patricia would be stuck behind bars where she belonged, and Angelica would be able to make fun of her.

Cooing at the doggies again, she said, "You know, I do have several ideas lined up, but I think Spider Williams might kill her and toss the body overboard. I truly do and who could blame him? However, if she survives the encounter, I have something equally delicious for her to tackle next."

Anna and Georgie, a little confused about recent events and their current location, nevertheless wagged their tails as the woman cooed in their faces.

Lady Obedience

I couldn't tell whether the man I was looking at was Spider Williams, aging rock star with a jaded past, or not because he was wearing a gas mask. Mercifully, I guess, it wasn't the only thing he was wearing. The man's nether region was clad in skin-tight, bright red PVC pants, and he had black PVC, four-inch spike heeled boots on his feet that came up to mid-thigh. He was also suspended three feet off the deck in a leather harness that itself was suspended from the ceiling.

Spider Williams had some preferences that strayed a little from the path I choose to walk.

"Mistress!" he squealed upon seeing me enter the bedroom. "I have been bad. Very bad." He had to tip his head way back and to the side to see me, and having done so, he said, "Hey, you're not Mistress Snapwhip."

Gritting my teeth, I growled, "Mistress Snapwhip is not available. She sent me instead. I'm … um." My brain wouldn't supply a name. I could have just left it blank, but too late now, I had to come up with something on the spot, or he was going to question why I didn't know my own name. "I'm Lady Obedience," I tried hopefully, wincing because it sounded daft once it left my mouth.

"But …"

"Silence!" I had no idea if my tone or attitude were right. I was basing the entire dominatrix persona on a few fleeting characters I'd caught on TV or in films, and on a thriller book I should have read the blurb for prior to making the purchase because it scarred me enough that I hid it in my freezer and never finished it.

I had been terrified about attempting to get into Spider Williams' suite, but not only was I now in his bedroom, he was completely at my mercy. On top of that, he had already admitted he was a bad boy, and with a heady rush of excitement, my flagging brain reminded me that I had a recording device in my possession.

Every modern phone had such functions loaded as basic background apps.

Feeling his eyes on me as I fiddled in my handbag, I boldly stated, "Phone to silent," so he would know what I was doing and genuinely flicked the little button to stop it ringing or beeping. Of course I also set the audio recording app to start working.

"Now then, worm," I strode around the room, trying to get into the feel of my character and keeping out of sight so he couldn't see how much my hands were shaking. "What evil, vile thing have you done?"

"Um."

"Don't mumble!" I spat my response before he had a chance to speak.

"Um, you're supposed to spank me every time I speak," he added, his voice sounding genuinely hopeful.

Now, I don't think of myself as a prude, but when it comes to the bedroom, I'm a traditional kinda gal. I go to church, and I know the Bible and I do not recall there being any passages about Abraham getting spanked by Sarah. I suppose that might have been what happened in Sodom and Gomorrah - I seem to recall my Sunday School teacher skipping hastily over those parts.

My point is I've never spanked anyone before. Nor have I ever been spanked for that matter, unless one counts an occasional playful smack on the rump that Alistair sneakily delivers when no one, including me, is paying attention.

I could see, however, that refusing to do so now was going to arouse suspicion. Did I really want to touch his backside with my bare hand though?

No. I did not.

Frantically looking around the room, I spotted a riding crop on his nightstand next to a pair of silver eggs – I had no idea what purpose they served - and a pair of tiny handcuffs.

Unable to help myself, when I picked up the riding crop, I also snagged the tiny handcuffs.

"What are these for?" I asked, truly curious.

Even with the gasmask on I could see his raised eyebrow.

"They're testicle handcuffs."

I let them slide from my fingers and onto the bed, looking around for something I could use to sterilise my hand.

"Ewww."

"What's going on?" Spider demanded. "Where's Mistress Whipsnap? She never said anything about not being available when I booked her earlier."

"Silence, worm! Don't question me!" To emphasise my instructions, I lashed out with the riding crop, whacking his left buttock with significantly more effort than I intended.

"Yow!" he squealed.

I whacked him on the bum again.

"Yow!"

The bedroom door burst open, the henchman/bodyguard coming through it.

"Everything all right, boss?" His eyes were flitting between the aging rocker, me, and the riding crop which I was swishing menacingly through the air because I liked the ziiiip noise it made.

"Is it?" I poked Spider on the side of his chin with the tip of the riding crop. "Is everything all right, worm? Do you require further correction?"

Spider wailed, "No! No, Mistress. But we haven't discussed tonight's safety word yet. I almost needed it then, but I don't have one."

I opened my mouth to ask him what on earth a safety word was, and only just managed to stop from giving myself away.

Whipping the riding crop through the air to point it at the bodyguard, I said, "Get out. Or strip, you little maggot, then crawl over here to beg for forgiveness."

I was so into the role now that it hadn't occurred to me what reaction my demand might bring. The bodyguard lowered himself to the carpet, bowed his head and started to pull at his tie.

Oh, my God, he was going to take off his clothes!

Spider twisted his head around to stare at his henchman. "Hey! What do you think you're doing? I'm paying for this session. Get out."

I whacked him on the rump because it seemed like the right thing to do.

"Yow!" His whole body tensed this time, his head arching back. "How about Oklahoma? That can be the safety word. Oklahoma! Oklahoma!"

"I'm giving the orders, worm," I sneered. "And you'll get a safety word when I think you've earned one."

Spider mumbled something and almost earned himself another strike from the riding crop. I wanted to get rid of the bodyguard though – getting to the deck he had knocked over my handbag with his foot. If he noticed, he might pick it up and I couldn't risk that he might see I was recording everything being said.

To the bodyguard, I said, "Get out. Wait for me as I instructed, and we shall see if you are worthy of punishment when I am finished here."

Without making eye contact, he backed out of the room.

My heart was still beating at five times its resting rate and making me feel really quite lightheaded. Incredibly, though, I not only felt in control, I was also beginning to believe I could pull this off.

I walked around the bed to where I had placed my handbag, collecting it and peering inside to find the little electronic voice recorder thing.

"What are you doing?" Spider asked, straining his head to see.

Thinking fast, I snapped my head around to glare at him.

"You just won't learn, will you, worm?"

"I'm just curious, Lady Obedience," he apologised quickly. "It's just … well, you're doing so well. I don't think I've ever had anyone dominate me quite as masterfully as you."

"Is that right?" I replied, masking my movements by taking out a lipstick I spotted rolling around at the bottom of my handbag. "I've never had to tolerate such a vile, despicable worm before." The phone was still working, the counter on the screen ticking off the seconds.

"What are you doing now?" he asked a moment later, twisting his head around in a bid to see.

It was a question worth asking, for I was using the lipstick, a soft pastel pink, to scrawl on his back.

"I am labelling you."

"I …"

I cut him off instantly. "Silence!" and whacked his bum again for good measure.

"Yow! Oklahoma! Oklahoma! Please, I need a safety word!"

Coming around to his head end, I grabbed the round bit of the gas-mask in front of his mouth and gave it a tug, moving his head from side to side.

"You will earn a safety word if you answer my questions and I like what I hear."

When I released his mask, he bowed his head. "Yes, mistress."

"Jolly good. You have been a bad man, haven't you, Spider Williams?"

"Yes, mistress."

"You have performed vile, unspeakable acts, haven't you?"

"Yes, mistress."

"You are a guilty man, aren't you, Spider Williams?"

"Yes, mistress."

"State your name." I wanted there to be no ambiguity on the recording.

"Hmmm? What was that?"

I raised the riding crop, but I didn't have to swing it. The sound of it parting the air on the way up was enough.

"William Harold Williams!" Spider blurted as fast as he could. "That's my real name. That's what it says on my birth certificate. Spider was the name my publicist came up with when I signed my first contract. They said William just didn't cut it." The confession about his name came in a torrent of words. If I could keep him talking like that, I could get all the details about how he killed his victim and arranged for the witness to 'disappear'.

That would stick it to Angelica. She'd sent me in here expecting it to result in all kinds of trouble for me. Or she just wanted to prove a point and have me fail. I doubted she had any idea about Spider's sexual preferences, that was just fate messing with me. Emerging victorious wouldn't do me any favours, if anything it would rile Angelica and make her even more spiteful, but it sure would make me feel better.

"Now tell me what you are guilty of!" I raged at him, the riding crop still high above my head and poised to descend.

"I'm a man!" he snivelled pathetically. "A worthless worm of a man."

That wasn't what I had hoped to hear.

"Yes, but more specifically, what crime have you committed? What heinous crime do you need to be punished for?"

Spider lifted his head. "Huh?"

I licked my lips nervously. I wasn't doing what he expected. Or I wasn't doing it right? I couldn't tell, but something was making him suspicious again.

"Your crime!" I commanded. "Shout it out so I can hear your confession! Tell me who you killed."

I got utter silence in return.

Two seconds passed, and just when I was about to whip my riding crop down on his buttocks, I discovered the thing that I had failed to notice.

Busted!

- -

L eft to strap himself into the harness, he had managed his ankles and his left wrist, but his right hand was as free as a bird. He had merely been resting it in the strap designed to trap it.

His right arm shot out to grab mine, trapping my right wrist in a steel grip.

"What's going on?" Spider demanded. "Where's Mistress Whipsnap? Why are you asking about who I killed?"

"Let go of me, worm!" I snapped.

"You're not a dominatrix at all, are you?" Spider concluded correctly.

Before I could answer, a commotion came from outside the bedroom door, and it burst open a moment later. I expected to see the body-guard again, but was unpleasantly surprised to find a petite Chinese woman glaring at me. That she was the real Mistress Whipsnap could be in little doubt for she was dressed in thigh high black PVC boots, and matching knickers and bra.

She'd arrived in a trench coat that covered her outfit, but it was discarded on the carpet behind her already. Her long, black hair was teased into a top knot that cascaded down her back to below her waist and she held a coiled bullwhip in her right hand.

I took the momentary distraction to rip my arm from Spider's grasp, but I never took my eyes away from the dangerous expression dominating (see what I did there?) the real dominatrix's face.

Both hands were balled and on her hips.

Spider cried, "Mistress Whipsnap!"

Her voice and mine rang in unison, "Silence worm!"

The bodyguard tried to get around the tiny Chinese lady who took offense to being barged, shooting a high elbow back into the man's face. His nose exploded as he tumbled backwards out of sight. I could hear him groaning and complaining, his words muffled.

It was just her and me now.

"Trying to steal my customers?" Mistress Whipsnap sneered. "What's an old hag like you doing in this profession anyway?"

"Old hag?" I thought that was a little harsh. Okay, I'm the wrong side of fifty, but still.

Spider was flailing at the strap holding his left wrist in place. He wanted to get free, and I could see how that would not work in my favour. I grabbed his one arm in both of mine and tried to wrestle it back to the open strap on the right hand side.

"I was just warming him up for you," I grunted from the effort of battling the crazy masochistic freak.

"She's a snitch! She's a snitch!" Spider shouted. "She was trying to get me to confess to murder."

I wasn't strong enough to get Spider's arm across the strap and Mistress Whipsnap was stalking across the bedroom with an angry grimace on her face. I doubted she was coming to give me a hand.

Taking my eyes off Spider proved to be a mistake, for in failing to control his arm he tore it from my grasp and his flailing limb caught me full in the mouth. It wasn't a punch, more like an accidental backhanded slap, but it burst my bottom lip, nevertheless.

I cried out and reeled away, holding a hand to my face as I tasted blood.

Spider tried to twist his head around to see where Mistress Whipsnap was, and with his free hand started to tear at the strap holding his left wrist in place.

"I'm gonna get you, you ... you fake dominatrix! I'm gonna beat a confession out of you! Who do you work for? Are you FBI? Interpol? Who is it?"

His left hand came free before I could stop him, but Mistress Whip-snap was coming around his feet and I was out of time anyway.

The look on her face suggested she intended violence, and given her chosen profession, I figured it was safe to assume she possessed few qualms about hurting people.

With only one avenue of escape, I leapt onto the bed, ran across it, and threw myself toward the door.

Spider roared his anger. "I'll give you fifty thousand dollars if you stop her!" I guess that offer was aimed at Mistress Whipsnap because he then shouted, "Ralph! Ralph! What are you doing? Get her!"

Ralph was just getting to the door when I burst through it, the opening edge of it smacking him in the face with enough force to send him reeling backwards. That I managed, inadvertently, to hit his nose which was already a bloody mess, was pure chance, but was the advantage I needed if I was going to escape.

I was moving so fast I had to lean to the left to stop myself from running into a wall. Ralph the bodyguard was down, and Spider was still trying to get free, but Mistress Whipsnap, a tiny minx less than half my age was giving pursuit and she was going to catch me in no time.

Bolting from the Hudson Suite into the passageway outside, I could hear her screaming abuse at my back in her native tongue. Chinese is such an elegant language to my ears, but I couldn't help guessing it was mostly cuss words and abuse I was hearing.

It changed in volume before I'd made it five yards, the nimble woman able to run in her insane heels and already gaining on me.

Echoing out from behind her, the voice of Spider Williams swore in a language I could understand. He was free of his binds and in pursuit too. Ralph had to be there somewhere though I wasn't about to risk a glance to check.

"I'm going to enjoy hurting you," shouted Mistress Whipsnap, the threat sending a chill down my spine.

I didn't have the confession Angelica sent me for. Did that mean she would hurt Anna or Georgie? I couldn't guess and there was nothing I could do about it right now.

Coming to the first intersection, I prayed the elevator around the corner might be ready for me. I wasn't sure I had enough time to get the doors closed before the dominatrix caught me, but maybe I would be able to shut us both inside and limit the pursuing trio to just one.

I heard Spider question where the expletive his expletive useless expletive other expletive bodyguard had expletive gone. The old rocker was in the passageway and running after me so had noticed the man positioned outside his suite door was missing.

He yelled several more expletives at my back as I jinked around the corner. Would I find people outside the elevator I could leverage for help? Maybe I would be truly in luck and there would be a couple of crewmembers from the security team standing around.

No. There were two kids.

They spun around to look at me, their eyes wide with shock that was changing to terror. To them I looked like a mad woman from a horror movie.

The youngest of the two – they were brothers given the similar facial features – had to be about six years old and he screamed like I was putting his fingers through a mangle.

He screamed a good deal louder when I swiped his scooter and ran off with it.

His older brother, just about into his teens, called me several names that would earn him a soapy mouthwash if he was my son, but I was already tearing down the passageway. Once I got the scooter under my feet, my pace increased dramatically.

Breathing hard – I might have said before that I am not a fan of being chased – I gasped in huge lungfuls of air and tried to stay in control of the death-trap on miniscule wheels.

The volume of Mistress Whipsnap's hurled abuses began to fade as I gained distance on her, so too the voices of Spider and Ralph. Allowing myself a moment to still my heartrate, I glanced over my shoulder to check how far behind they were.

Were they giving up? Had I managed to get away?

That a steward chose that moment to step out of an intersection should have been predictable, but my brain was already working on too many other quandaries to spare time on minutiae like the universe conspiring against me.

I don't know at what speed a child's scooter wheels catch fire and it travels back in time, but that's about how fast I was going when I slammed into the steward. It was a glancing blow, mercifully, me catching the worst of it when my face collided with his elbow.

He had his right arm high with a tray of drinks balanced on it. Bound for one of the suites no doubt, the tray toppled, and I crashed.

The poor steward spun in place, startled, out of control, and trying to keep his drinks from all crashing to the deck.

My face felt like I had run into a brick wall. The force of the blow had gone through my left cheekbone which now felt like it was on fire. Of course, my chasers saw the whole thing and doubled their speed in a bid to get to me before I could regain my feet.

"Hey! You there!"

On the deck with a bruised face and skinned knees, the sound of some-one new shouting made me look up. To my right were two members of the ship's security team. My first thought was that I was saved, but then it became apparent they were reacting to a call about the stolen scooter.

Word sure travels fast.

"You with the scooter. Stop right there!"

Both officers were young men – part of the new tranche of security officers we took on in Lanzarote. Their hands were already touching the butts of their sidearms, youthfulness and excitement fuelled by adrenalin proving to be a dangerous combination.

"She's trying to rob me!" shouted the steward, his panicked remark making me whip my head around to gawp at him. Only at that point did I discover I'd knocked the wallet from his tray, and it was on the floor by my knees. All stewards carry one in case passengers wish to pay with cash. They keep their tips in it too, and he thought I had crashed into him deliberately.

I scrambled to my feet.

"Hey!" yelled the young security officers from my right.

"Hey, you expletive expletive expletive!" shouted Spider from behind me.

Mistress Whipsnap screamed something too. I had no idea what it was, and I wasn't hanging around for a translator.

With the scooter back under my right foot, I kicked the wallet across the deck with my left. It fetched up against the toe of the steward's left foot and when he bent down to reclaim it, I snatched what looked to be a semi-spilled gin and tonic from the tray.

I threw it into my mouth, desperate for something to drink and wishing I was lazing in my bath with a supply of Hendricks on tap.

"Urrrgh, vodka lemonade," I spat, having swallowed the foul liquid. With a shudder and then a squeal of fright because everyone was converging on me, I set off again.

I needed my friends. Angelica be damned, I was being chased and might not live to reclaim my dogs depending on who caught me.

The two ensigns were babbling into their radios, sending instructions to be on the lookout for a crazy woman with bubble-gum hair, a stolen child's scooter, and a fat bum. I swear I almost stopped and went back to give him a piece of my mind at his inclusion of the final descriptor, but I had reached the next corner and was very thankfully getting out of sight.

The Man from HQ

L ieutenant Commander Martin Baker looked across at his wife Lieutenant Deepa Bhukari, his eyes filled with question.

"You don't think ..."

Deepa snorted a hopeless sigh of despair.

"Are you kidding, Martin? A madwoman who just stole a child's scooter, wearing a latex pink anime kitten outfit and being pursued by a dominatrix, a man with a severe facial injury and another man wearing a gas mask, a pair of latex pants, and spike heeled boots. If that's not Patricia Fisher, then she has a rival for unleashing chaos on board."

Martin's phone rang, Lieutenant Schneider's voice booming out of it when he thumbed the green button and put it on speaker.

"Guys, did you just hear that last transmission?"

Martin started running. "Get to the top deck! We'll meet you there!" They were on deck sixteen, following up on the note a hairdresser delivered to Patricia's suite less than fifteen minutes ago.

It wasn't a whole lot to go on, but the handwritten message from Mrs Fisher had provided them with some relief – she was keeping them in the game. The note was brief and scrawled in eyeliner, and it begged they hold back from getting directly involved as she knew they would want to, but asked them to be ready – like chess pieces – to strike if she needed.

She believed she was being followed and had provided a description. It still wasn't a lot to go on. Early twenties, Asian – that covered a lot of territory – tall and lean. They were going to do their best, but there was a lot of ship, a lot of passengers, and though they had a clue where Patricia had been a few minutes ago, they had not one clue where she was now.

In the Windsor Suite, Barbie, her injured left foot immobilised and resting on a cushion, was already looking through the extensive passenger manifest as she tried to narrow down the list of possible suspects for the young Asian man.

Her task was easier than that facing Martin and the others – they had to rely on blind luck to put them in the right place at the right time to then be able to spot the right man if he walked by. It was a long shot, but there was nothing to be gained by all six of them crowding around the computer screen when one person could do it.

She took a bite of an apple and scrolled to another image.

What she couldn't know, having narrowed the search down to those passengers who were male, under fifty, and not Caucasian, was that Jordan had hacked the ship's central registry the day he came aboard. He was listed as Afro-Caribbean and his picture, age, and passport details logged in the computer were all fake.

They were for a real person, just not one who was on the ship.

Barbie didn't know this, and blithely unaware how wily her target was, she scrolled to the next image, made a note that the man she saw vaguely fit the description they had, and moved on.

The knock at the door broke her concentration, but she didn't get up. So used to Jermaine answering the door, it didn't occur to her that he wasn't going to until a few seconds later when someone knocked again.

Only then did Barbie remember that Jermaine was out. He was with the others, doing his best to find Patty and keep her safe.

Stuck in a wheelchair and being good because she wanted her ankle to heal, Barbie wheeled herself across to the door, calling out, "Won't be a moment," because it was taking her so long to respond to whoever was outside.

She had to reverse up to the door so she could reach it and was surprised to find the captain outside.

"Sir?" she questioned. "Um, Mrs Fisher isn't here." Cursing the wheelchair and her elevated foot, she rolled herself back a foot so she could open the door more fully.

The voice of someone she hadn't seen remarked, "I rather hope she is out pursuing the report of a madwoman being chased by a dominatrix."

Captain Huntley stepped inside the lobby of the Windsor Suite as Barbie backed up a little more and she caught sight of the other person.

"Miss Berkeley, this is Mr Torrance," the captain explained. "He is here to conduct a review of the ship, its efficiency, the level of staff training, that sort of thing."

"And an assessment of Mrs Fisher's performance which has been the subject of much debate at Purple Star let me tell you," the man remarked, the timbre of his voice suggesting he already had a negative opinion on the subject.

Mr Torrance peered disapprovingly at Barbie through round-lensed spectacles that made his eyes look like those of an insect. He was short with thinning hair and bore the look of a person whose life revolved around spreadsheets and numbers. That he was forming a conclusion about Patty without even meeting her was apparent to Barbie and she didn't like it.

Automatically, she lied.

"She is indeed out pursuing the report, Sir. That is precisely what she is doing. Never one for resting is our Patricia."

"And what is your role?" Mr Torrance demanded to know, his eyes looking beyond Barbie's head and into the suite.

"I'm a fitness instructor."

Mr Torrance looked down at her injured foot, tapping the wheelchair with a toe to make a light clonging sound.

"Is that so?"

Barbie opened her mouth to speak, but the man from Purple Star HQ cut her off.

"You're blocking the way, girl. Move back."

Barbie hadn't deliberately chosen to wedge her wheelchair in the door leading from the lobby into the suite proper, but it was there never-theless, and Mr Torrance couldn't get past unless he was prepared to clamber over her.

Unused to being spoken down to, Barbie was about to give the little man from HQ a piece of her mind when the captain lifted an arm to block his path.

"I'm afraid not, Ian. Unless welcomed to enter, this is Patricia Fisher's suite," Alistair explained.

He got a derisive snort in reply. "Nonsense, man. We own the ship." He made to push the captain's arm aside and intended to do the same thing to the girl in the wheelchair, but the arm did not budge as he expected.

Calmly, Alistair said, "Purple Star Lines do not own this suite, Ian. They sold it to the Maharaja of Zangrabar in perpetuity for an undisclosed sum. I am sure you must have read about that in the minutes of one of your meetings."

Barbie applied the brake on her wheelchair and folded her arms.

"This is preposterous," Mr Torrance protested. "Well, then I want to know where Mrs Fisher is. There are unacceptable occurrences taking place on board the cruise line's finest vessel and she was employed to prevent them from happening."

"Almost correct," replied Alistair, his voice calm and matter of fact. "Mrs Fisher is the ship's detective and expected to investigate after the fact. She is not expected to predict crimes and make arrests before they happen. She can only react when events occur."

Mr Torrance ran out of argument, but the sense that he was dissatisfied was apparent. He spun around on his heels, leaving the suite's lobby without another word.

Barbie got a friendly nod from her captain before he too departed, closing the door behind him.

Left alone in the palatial cabin, Barbie worried, "Oh, Patty. Where are you?"

I Gave You One Job

Angelica was proud of her scowling face. It had been well employed in her life and was aimed directly at Jordan now.

"What do you mean you lost her?" she demanded to know. "I gave you one job."

Jordan felt like a naughty schoolboy summoned before the headmistress and he hated it.

"I followed her to the salon like you said and made sure she was wearing the outfit and had her hair looking how you wanted."

Angelica had been pleased with that part of his task. She'd watched Patricia leaving the salon and saw the looks she was getting from the people around her. She looked memorably idiotic. This did little to detract from Jordan's subsequent failure though. He was supposed to keep her in sight at all times.

It was necessary because the ship's CCTV feed - which Jordan hacked into and had set up on a network of ten different monitors in the tiny cabin – needed someone to first know roughly where she was. There were too many cameras viewing the public areas for it to ever be possible for a person to watch them all. Jordan, therefore, was deployed to watch her and relay to Angelica where to look.

The pink hair and kitten ears were going to make it so much easier to spot her in a crowd, yet Angelica had lost Patricia all the same and it was all Jordan's fault for letting her give him the slip.

"Yes. So what happened then?" Angelica scowled some more.

Jordan squirmed. "She went to the Hudson Suite as expected and I waited out of sight so I would see when she left."

"Yes," Angelica encouraged, though her expression told Jordan she was walking him into a trap.

He was getting annoyed at how he was always in the weaker position. Patricia Fisher escaping him wasn't his fault. He'd tried to keep up, but that wasn't something Angelica would care about. She wasn't interested in effort, only in results.

Well, there were things she didn't know.

"She knocked out the bodyguard, you know."

Angelica's expression froze, but only for a second. "Poppycock. Don't be so ridiculous, Jordan. How could she have possibly?"

"Well," Jordan started. "It was sort of a reverse headbutt." Seeing the doubt and confusion on Angelica's face, he stepped back a pace and mimed what happened. "She fell over, and when he got close enough, she threw her head up into his face. Honestly, it was a sweet move. It reminded me of watching Jackie Chan when he fights people, but pretends to be drunk."

Angelica had no idea what the young idiot was saying and was utterly certain he was making it up. She wanted to cross examine him to get to the truth, but chose instead to make him press on with his story and listen as he got confused by his own lies.

"What happened after her supposed reverse headbutt then?"

Back on less shaky ground, Jordan explained about the three ladies who turned up to carry the unconscious bodyguard away. Angelica stopped him when he got to the part about the dominatrix.

"A dominatrix?"

"That's what she looked like to me. Smoking hot body too ..." his sentence drifted off the road and crashed when he caught the look Angelica was giving him. "That's definitely what she was because when Mrs Fisher came out of the suite about two minutes later, she was running, and the dominatrix was chasing her and so was Spider Williams."

Jordan had never heard of Spider Williams until earlier today. He was just too young to be familiar with his music, but admitted he'd seen the story on the TV news a while ago. Angelica had insisted on making him listen to several of the geriatric rocker's greatest hits. It just sounded like garbage to Jordan and about as tuneful as listening to a herd of flatulent cows.

"How is that proof that she was a dominatrix?" Angelica demanded.

"Because Spider Williams had on spike heels, a pair of latex pants and a full head gasmask!" He pulled out his phone to show her the picture he'd taken.

Somewhat taken aback, not least because Jordan hadn't been lying after all, Angelica pressed on.

"This still doesn't explain how you lost sight of Patricia Fisher."

Bored, and mentally plotting his escape from Angelica's employment, Jordan explained about the scooter, more members of the ship's security team arriving – the ones from Patricia Fisher's team no less - and the very real likelihood that he was going to get caught up in the confusing bedlam Patricia Fisher left in her wake. He didn't want to be answering questions to the ship's security team and Angelica didn't want that either.

Reluctantly she let him off the hook.

"You are going to need to be ready to follow her again. When she tells me where she is, your job is to keep her in sight."

Seeing Angelica reach for her phone, Jordan said, "Ah, I don't think she has her phone with her."

"What?"

"Yeah, sorry. She had her handbag when she went into the Hudson Suite, but it wasn't with her when she came out again."

Angelica tried it, nevertheless, cursing and swearing when Patricia failed to keep up.

"Fisher!" she raged. "Where are you!"

On the Run

My flight from Spider, Ralph, and Mistress Whipsnap only ended because the security guards got in their way. Losing them, however, did little to improve my situation. Now I was being hounded by the ship's security guards. Scooting away with my lungs searing and my thighs protesting, I'd heard their radio messages bringing more of them into the pursuit.

They didn't know it was me and I was leaving it that way. I was going to be easy to catch though, my outfit kind of stood out. Getting out of sight was a priority.

I found the first stairwell I could and got off the top deck, parking the scooter where I hoped it would be found.

If you are on the top deck, there is no up you can go to which made predicting my route far easier for anyone pursuing me. I had to get down a few decks and hope that by doing so I could lose the chasing pack.

I made it to deck seventeen before I even considered slowing down. Until then I had been keeping to the outer passageways – the ones I knew would only have passengers in them if they were coming or going from their cabins. Now, I shifted inward to the entertainment areas, losing myself among the press of passengers still enjoying all the ship had to offer. The pools were closed at this time of the evening and so were most of the shops, but bars, cinemas, restaurants, and clubs were all in full swing.

There were still children about, their parents making exception to normal bedtimes because there was no school tomorrow and it meant they got to stay out and have a drink too.

It was good for me because I was going to be harder to spot, but I was getting looks. The outfit was something else, and the bubble-gum pink hair just made it worse. The fat lip wasn't going to help my cause and I had to question whether the blow to my cheek had left a mark because my cheekbone still throbbed from impacting the steward's elbow.

Did I have a black eye? I gasped and touched my face. Then stopped to look in the window of a shop that had closed for the night. Twisting my head left and right as I tried to catch enough light to see the damage in the reflection, I couldn't be sure if I had bruising to my face or not, but I thought maybe I did.

A black eye. My first ever.

A flash of white to my left caught my eye, the distinctive uniform of the ship's security team. Since the day I came on board the Aurelia, with very few exceptions, having those white uniforms by my side had been a comfort.

Right now, they were anything but.

I believed I had lost the young man I suspected to be following and watching me, but that wasn't as comforting as it ought to have been. That Angelica knew I was lying about which deck I was on earlier troubled me. How could there have been someone following me already? If it was a bug in my phone, then Angelica would think I was still in the Hudson Suite.

Running over the bed to get away from Mistress Whipsnap, there just wasn't a way for me to get my handbag. It was still there now and would be found when Spider returned.

I knew I wasn't supposed to have any contact with my friends, but would Angelica know if I went back to my suite? It hadn't occurred to me to head that way when I ran from Spider, but I could circle around to go there now.

The white uniforms were coming closer, and they had to know to be on the lookout for someone matching my description.

Ruled by indecision, I backed into an alcove where I was out of sight and could think. From there, I looked around for a direction I could go. What would happen if I simply turned myself in? I am Patricia

Fisher, the ship's detective after all. Once they knew who I was, the situation would quickly resolve itself.

But what if Angelica found out? No help. That was her instruction. I was already worried she might see Marsha's assistance as something which broke the rules, but it was too late for me to undo what had transpired outside Spider's cabin.

With no phone on which I could contact Angelica or be contacted by her, I was going to have to get my handbag back and it was with that in mind that I began to make my way back to my suite. I could see no path for me to accomplish the retrieval of my phone by myself, but Jermaine could get it. I was going to have to ask for his help and pray that Angelica didn't find out.

However, the moment I stepped out from my hiding place, I found yet another pair of security guards coming my way. This pair were coming right for me, and I knew who they were – Lieutenants Harvey and Nichols. They still held a grudge against me for having them stripped naked and locked in the brig a few months ago. It was their own fault it happened, but they saw me, and whether they recognised who it was beneath the costume or not, they started running.

I squealed in alarm and darted through the crowd. All around me, passengers were contently going about their evening, enjoying themselves and undoubtedly looking forward to the rest of their days on board.

They were utterly unaware of the drama playing out right next to them, though I got a few glances as I dashed by. To be fair, the glances might have been just because I looked deranged in my daft costume.

Shooting my head around to the left, I could see white uniforms converging on me. One man had a hand on his radio, transmitting my location to bring even more of his colleagues my way.

One advantage that came from having been on the ship for so long was that I knew my way around. Just ahead was a door that led to a passage to the storerooms behind the shops. On the door was a sign advising 'Crew Only' but it was never locked, the continual crew traffic coming in and out made locking it impractical.

I ducked as I ran, utilising the greater height of the people around me to hide my movements. Would it work? There was no way to mask the door opening and closing, but I ran past it, popped up to make myself visible so they would think I was continuing in that direction, then quickly doubled back.

When I slid through the door, Harvey and Nichols were close enough that I could hear the tinny voices coming over their radios. I put my weight against it, looking for a locking mechanism I could turn.

There wasn't one. If they saw where I went or figured it out, I was as good as caught.

I held my breath, staring at the door as I backed away.

The door blocked out ninety percent of the noise from outside, but I heard it when Lieutenant Harvey said, "Where did she go?"

It wasn't going to take them long to figure out where I was. Panicking, I spun around, looking for a direction to run. The passageway stretched into the distance, a straight line ending in a bulkhead, however there were doors on both sides. I snatched at a handle, finding it locked and refusing to budge.

I tried another with the same result.

"Hey, maybe she went in here." I heard the voice of Lieutenant Nichols and saw the door at the end of the passageway beginning to open.

I was a heartbeat away from being caught, but just when I thought I might as well accept defeat, I spotted that the next door was ajar. I threw myself at it, yanking it open and diving through the gap. Someone had jammed a piece of card between the door and the frame to keep it open. I flicked that out of the way and pulled the door shut a fraction of a second before I heard a voice in the passageway outside.

Lieutenant Nichols said, "Doesn't look like it."

"How the heck did we lose her?" Harvey asked.

I wanted to hold my breath, I was gasping lungfuls and would swear I was making so much noise they couldn't fail to hear me. They didn't though, silence returning to the passageway outside when they closed the door leading to the seventeenth deck shopping precinct.

I waited five minutes, terrified they might have been savvy enough to leave one man standing silently in the passageway in case I appeared. Then, when I'd counted off five minutes in my head, I gave it another five just to be sure. I was in a storeroom for one of the gift shops, the space behind me filled with shelves on which boxes of souvenirs were stacked.

"Okay, Patricia, they've gone," I told myself, speaking aloud because the quiet was beginning to unnerve me. With a deep breath, I gripped the door handle and turned it.

Except it didn't.

It didn't budge.

I applied some more pressure, adding my other hand as the inescapable truth of my situation hit home.

I was locked in.

That was why there had been a piece of card wedged in the door jam. The lock was broken, or they left it this way because it was faster – it autolocked, and the staff using this storeroom couldn't be bothered to keep opening it with a key each time they needed something.

I wanted to feel sorry for myself, but truly my thoughts were only for Anna and Georgie, my two dachshunds. They were being held at the mercy of a lunatic bent on making my life into a living hell. If you had asked me a month ago if Angelica Howard-Box was capable of harming a living creature, I would have replied with a firm 'No'. Now I wasn't so sure.

With no option I could see, I called for help, filling my lungs with air, and shouting as loudly as I could.

Though I strained my hearing to listen, no answer came back. No one heard me and no one was coming to let me out. Not until the morning when the shops opened again.

I cursed my luck. I might have no idea what anyone else is doing, but I did know I was trapped.

Barbie

The search for the young Asian man was not going well. Martin, Deepa, and the others had responded to an incident that was almost certainly of Patty's making, but she was long gone by the time they got there. They searched the area, but found no sign of a young Asian man either and no one who could recall seeing a man who might even loosely fit the description Patty gave them earlier.

Catching him on foot had always been a long shot though which was why Barbie had put off the other tasks on her list to focus on identifying him.

On the passenger manifest there were six hundred and fifty-four Asian men from a variety of different nations. That was after her initial filter where she took out anyone over forty. She then segregated the list further by placing anyone travelling with a family or significant other into an 'unlikely' pile. It left her with three men, all of which were about to get a visit from Lieutenant Commander Baker and his team.

There was nothing else she could do to help Patty for now, but Barbie wasn't about to let that stop her from working – there were other mysteries yet to be researched. The one at the top of the list was Professor Noriega.

That a researcher from a prestigious museum would attack her and Patty at knifepoint was shocking and Barbie, touching the piece of sticking plaster covering the small cut his blade made in the flesh of her throat, wanted to know why he had done it.

The man jumped through a window and escaped when Hideki, Big Ben, and Jermaine burst through a wall to rescue her and Patty. The ship had been due to sail, removing the option to pursue the professor across the island. They filed a report with the local police, but the man who took their details had just been reinstated ten years after retiring – the police on the island were in utter disarray, so Barbie held little hope that anything productive would be done. Or even attempted.

At first, she thought the professor would be stuck on the island and that Patricia would be able to get someone there to investigate on her behalf. However, the moment she typed his name into the search bar and pressed enter, all previous concepts regarding Professor Noriega went out the window.

She stared at the screen, her mouth open and her coffee going cold while she read the report at the top of the page with utter disbelief.

Professor Noriega of the Museum of Brazil was dead. He'd been dead for more than a week and he looked nothing like the Professor Noriega she'd met.

She had no idea what that meant, but it wasn't anything good.

After more than a minute gawping at the news article, which went on to explain that the Professor's research assistant had died the previous day in an unrelated accident, Barbie started a new search.

The fake Professor Noriega had been interested in just one thing, the albino stowaway and the uncut gems found in his belly. Barbie bit her bottom lip and strained to remember what he had said at breakfast when they first met him. There was something about …

"Shipwreck!" she blurted aloud though there was no one in the suite to hear her. The man – whoever he was – had talked about the possibility the gems had come from a ship hauling treasure from the new world back to Europe. Her knowledge of that part of world history was sparse – history in general hadn't been a subject she'd given much attention to at school, but with time to kill and nothing better to do, she created a new file, called it 'Titanic' for obvious reasons and started to jot notes as she searched the internet for whatever information she could find.

Barbie didn't have a lot to go on, but the coins had to be a clue. They gave her a year and that gave her an era. She also knew they were Spanish.

Mentally cracking her knuckles, the Californian blonde stretched her back and rolled her shoulders – it was going to be a long night.

Knife Edge

I awoke in a bewildered daze, flipping over in bed when Jermaine opened the door to my bedroom. The sudden and unexpected feeling of gravity snatching at my body made me squeal and it was only when I hit the cold deck that I came to my senses.

"What the heck?" asked the young woman now staring down at me. She had her right hand clasped to her heart as she recovered from the shock of finding me inside the storeroom.

I was covered in towels and had to fight my way out of them. Unhappily accepting my fate the previous evening, I'd explored the shelves until I found a box containing souvenir towels. Embossed with the Purple Star Cruise Line's logo and with a stitched image of the Aurelia in one corner, the bath sheets were put to good use as a bed on one of the lower shelves once I cleared it.

I wouldn't claim it had been comfortable, but with the fatigue from my eventful visit to the British Union Isles, I had slept right through until this morning.

Assuming, that is, that it was now morning.

"What time is it?" I begged, fumbling with the towels as I clambered to my feet.

I didn't get an answer, I got questions instead.

"Who are you? What are you doing in the storeroom?" Then her tone changed as her brain kicked in. "I need to call security."

She was backing out of the room and swinging the door shut. I had to throw the bundle of towels in my hands so they jammed the door and stopped it from shutting. That bought me the two seconds I needed to get across the room and force the door open.

The young woman outside was shoving it closed, her weight against it while she tried to yank the towels clear.

"I'm calling security!" she shouted. "Help! Help!"

"Please," I begged, bracing a foot against a shelf and using it to give me the leverage I needed to push the door open. "You don't understand."

With a final shove, I lunged for the gap. Naturally, I tripped on the towels and fell on my face, but I was outside in the passageway once more.

Rolling over, I used my hands to show that I was surrendering and offered the woman a smile. She had a name badge with 'Kim' displayed on it.

"Kim, I'm Patricia Fisher. The Ship's Detective. I'm sure you've heard of me. I'm dating the captain."

"Oh, yeah?" Kim challenged. "What were you doing in the storeroom all night then? I've heard of Patricia Fisher. Everyone has, but she doesn't look like you. She's elegant ..." I liked that, "and English and she doesn't dress like a ... like a ... what the heck are you wearing anyway?"

I kept my hands at chest height to show I was no threat as I got to my feet and looked down at my ridiculous outfit.

"I think it's supposed to be an anime kitten outfit?" I hazarded, genuinely unsure exactly what it might have been originally listed as. Looking back up so I met Kim's eyes, I said, "I was investigating a case and got trapped in here last night. Someone was chasing me. This outfit is a disguise."

Kim skewed her lips to one side, considering my claim. After a moment, she said, "That does sound like the sort of thing I have heard about Mrs Fisher. You do look like her too, now that I can see your face a bit better." She peered inside the storeroom. "You've been in there all night?"

I sighed, ready to get on my way. "Yes. I guess I've slept in worse places."

Kim bit her lip, an excited sparkle in her eyes all of a sudden.

"Can I ask a question?"

"Um, I guess." I was looking at the door to take me back out to the deck seventeen shopping precinct. I wanted to go, but Kim had just granted me my freedom and though I had no idea what she wanted to know, I doubted indulging her would delay me for more than a few seconds.

"What's the captain like in bed?" Kim's wide-eyed expression expected an answer, and she was all ears to hear what I had to say. "He's got such a nice bum," she added.

"Oh, wow, um, sorry," I stuttered, heat rising in my cheeks. This was not a subject I was happy to discuss with anyone. Probably not even Alistair. "I, ah ... I can't say I have any complaints," I managed. "Sorry, I really have to go." I backed toward the exit, and then remembered the towels and my makeshift bed. "Sorry about the mess."

Kim flapped a dismissive arm at me. "Don't worry. I'll leave it for Darren. He deserves it."

I thanked her again and left her behind, sneaking out onto the concourse of shops I'd last seen many hours ago. I never did get an answer from her on what time it was, but from the number of people I could see it had to be quite early in the day still, somewhere around breakfast time.

As you might imagine, the first task on my list was to find a restroom. I'd been stuck in the storeroom all night with no way to deal with any personal needs. Two minutes later, with the necessary task behind me,

I was heading for my suite. I had to make contact with Angelica and for that I needed to get the burner phone and for that I needed Jermaine. Or someone.

It didn't have to be Jermaine; Barbie could charm her way into any heterosexual man's cabin. The wheelchair, much like anyone else who was more permanently fixed to such a device, did nothing to diminish her beauty.

However, as I hurried on my way, and climbed aboard an escalator as part of my ascent through the ship, who did I see coming down on the other side? None other than Spider Williams.

I hit the deck. Or rather, I flung myself painfully to the surface of the escalator, doing so with such disregard for its solid and unyielding nature that I had to stuff a fist in my mouth to stifle my own cries of pain.

Still dressed exactly as I had been the previous evening, there was no way Spider and his bodyguard, Ralph, wouldn't see me. Spider was wearing a white shirt and a pale Panama hat above light blue cotton trousers – a vast improvement on last night's wardrobe choices.

I clung to the step, getting odd looks from the couple a few steps above me and concern from a man who joined the escalator behind me. He was carrying a bag of what had to be breakfast to take back to his cabin. The thought made my stomach growl hungrily.

"Are you okay?" he asked, racing up the steps to get to me. "Here, let me give you a hand up."

I slapped his hand away.

The man recoiled with surprise, his face showing the shock he felt, until a frown formed. He was about to snap something at me when I apologised.

"Sorry," I hissed. "I'm hiding from someone."

He looked up and around. "Who?"

"Shhhh!" I put a finger to my lips, begging him to be quiet. He was drawing attention to the fact that there was someone on the escalator who was very clearly staying out of sight, and my brain was telling me Spider Williams and Ralph had to be passing me right about now.

I wanted to take a peek, but stayed clinging to the escalator instead. In fact, I stayed there so long, watching down the steps to the deck below so I would see when Spider walked away, that I was still there when the step I was on reached the top and started to level out.

With a jolt, I realised I needed to get up, but by then it was, of course, too late. I twisted around and grabbed for the handrail, but the frill y ruffles under my skirt were trapped between my step and the one before it and I was heading for the knife edge where the deck eats the steps.

"Arrrrgh!" I squealed, on my knees and tearing at my skirt to free it. Was I going to lose my skirt and be forced go the rest of the way in my knickers? Or was that the best-case scenario I ought to be hoping for because I was to get chopped in half? "Arrrgh, help!"

The young man with his bag of breakfast hooked two hands under my armpits and hauled skyward, lifting me from the surface of the escalator just before the knife edge showed me what it could do with human flesh when given the chance. The ruffly stuff ripped, a chunk of it vanishing under the knife edge as the young man stepped onto deck eighteen holding me in the air.

I sucked in an adrenalin filled gasp and slowly lowered my feet to the deck.

My rescuer asked, "Are you okay?"

A small crowd of curious passengers forming around us as the escalator delivered more of them right behind us and those on deck eighteen took an interest.

A man said, "You look like you had a wild night, lady." He was in his sixties and clearly found my predicament amusing.

More sympathetic, his wife asked, "Are you in any trouble?" She was looking at my swollen lip and the black eye I suspected was there.

I bowed my head, looking at the deck so it made the marks of my face less easy to see.

"I'm fine," I replied. It wasn't exactly a lie. Sure, I was being emotionally tortured by a crazy woman who had stolen my dogs and was threatening to drop them overboard, and I was cut off from my friends, hadn't eaten in twelve hours, needed a shower, and slept on a shelf using towels as a pillow and a blanket, but there wasn't actually anything wrong with me. Nothing that the concerned persons around me could fix for sure.

I knew the crowd would attract the attention of security who would still be on the lookout for a woman matching my description. Above all else, I needed to get away from the people around me and avoid being spotted until I could get back to my suite and change.

"Really, I'm fine," I repeated, pushing my way through the press of passengers around me. Comments were being made. Questions too as those who saw me wondered what the heck I was wearing and why I looked like I had slept in my clothes. A few suggested I was doing the walk of shame after hooking up with some random man the previous evening. I ignored them all, scurrying away and exiting the area through the first door I came to.

I wanted to get to my cabin. Even though Angelica was adamant I wasn't allowed to have my friends help me, I needed to get cleaned up and there was no way she had anyone tailing me now. One thing I didn't need was help to retrieve my phone. Spider and Ralph were out of the Hudson Suite and the one thing I still had in my possession was Spider's key card.

Fresh Accusations

The Hudson Suite was kind of on the way to my own cabin if I took a small detour. Obviously, that's precisely what I did, acting like I had every right to open the door and go inside when I arrived there.

I called out once I had the door open, checking to make sure the other bodyguard, the one Marsha carried off, hadn't returned. I got silence in reply, counted to three while I listened for the sound of a person hiding out of sight, decided I was being silly and ran to Spider's bedroom.

My handbag wasn't where I'd left it, but had been kicked under the bed at some point, probably when Spider and Mistress Whipsnap chased me from the room.

A quick check assured me everything important was still in it, but more than anything I wanted the phone. The screen showed dozens of missed calls and messages from Angelica, her tone becoming ever more threatening and angry as she continued to get no response.

The battery had the tiniest bar of red showing – it had been on all night, recording whatever sounds Spider might have made. It was going to die soon without a charge, but I was going to make a call anyway.

"Patricia!" Angelica snapped into my ear. "Why has it taken you this long to answer me?"

Huffing a breath as I fought to keep my anger under control, I said, "I was trapped in a storeroom all night. I would have called you if I could have. I had to wait until the staff opened up again this morning." I wanted to complain that her daft demands had almost got me killed – I'm not sure what Spider might have done to me if he'd been given a chance. Obviously, I chose not to waste my breath; Angelica would probably be delighted if I got myself killed.

"Did you succeed in extracting a confession from Spider Williams?"

A snort escaped my nose. "No, Angelica. Of course I didn't."

"Because you are a liar and a fraud," she sneered with satisfaction. "I knew you would fail if truly tested. Don't worry though, your next task will be easier."

"Next task," I muttered. "This is crazy Angelica. I've done what you asked. I've quit my job. I've made myself look ridiculous. Give me back my dogs!"

My demand triggered an instant change in tone and volume as she roared, "No! You have so much further to fall yet, Patricia Fisher. I will give you back your dogs when I decide it is time, not when you demand it."

In a quiet voice that was as close to pleading as I was going to get, I asked, "Have you hurt my dogs?"

Angelica chuckled, "Wouldn't you like to know?"

With the phone against my left ear, I used my right hand to close the door to the Hudson Suite behind me as I left. Growling my reply, I said, "I need proof that they are okay, Angelica. I want to know that you haven't hurt them. Show me my dogs, please. I'm not doing a thing until I know they are still alive."

She didn't reply straight away, taking a few seconds to decide whether to concede to my request.

After a few seconds and just when I was thinking I needed to beg, she said, "Very well. I'm taking a picture of them right now."

I heard the fake shutter click modern phones employ so the user knows the camera function is operating and a few seconds later, a text message pinged into my phone. Anna and Georgie were on a bed looking up at the phone. They were unharmed and the time stamp on the picture was just a few seconds old.

They were okay, my heart aching with worry that anything could ever happen to them.

I said, "Thank you," though I wasn't sure if I meant it. In truth, while my heart ached with the need to get my dogs back into my care, my brain saw more than just them in the picture. I needed time to check on something …

Angelica's voice broke my concentration and when she spoke again, her tone was laced with venom. "They are unharmed, Patricia. How long they stay like that is down to you. I have a new task for you and the clock is ticking. When we arrive in Rio, I will be leaving the ship, so your time is limited. If you want your dogs back, you are going to have to earn their release."

I bit down against the bile rising in my throat.

"What do you want me to do Angelica?"

I listened with incredulity, the insanity of her demand beyond anything I could have imagined.

"I'm not going to do that, Angelica!" I snapped. "Have you lost your mind?"

She chuckled as if it were funny. "Of course, Patricia. It is entirely your choice whether your dogs live or die."

The words I had ready for her died in my mouth. I was going to do what she said, and I knew it.

Quietly. reluctantly, I replied, "Okay, Angelica. I'll do it."

"Be sure that you do, Patricia. I shall be watching. Oh, and just to keep you on your toes, I've arranged a little added fun to make sure you don't try to enlist the help of your friends."

"Added fun?" I wanted to ask her what that meant, but Angelica had already hung up. "What could she have done now that would stop me getting help?

I messaged my tormentor, '*My phone battery is almost dead. I need to go back to my suite to charge it or you won't be able to send me instructions.*'

Her response was unexpected. '*Of course, Patricia.*'

She was cutting me a break. Ok, Angelica was only doing it because she wanted to make sure I was contactable, but I was taking it. Hurrying, my pace close to a jog, I made my way around the top deck. I was almost at my suite when I heard Alistair's voice.

A euphoric sense of relief and hope flashed through my body and mind. If I could hear him, then he was outside my suite and that meant he was getting involved. I could explain about the debacle last night and have him cancel the instruction to catch the woman in the daft pink anime kitten outfit.

However, just as my pace began to quicken, a tinge of doubt stopped me. I could hear his voice, but he was arguing.

"The report is false," he stated firmly.

His remark was answered by a voice I didn't know - that of a man, an American.

"You know that for sure, do you, Captain Huntley?" It was clearly a rhetorical question which the man answered for himself a moment later. "Of course not, which is why she is to be detained on sight and every member of the ship's security team must be on the lookout for her."

Alistair didn't have to think about his retort. "I am in command on this ship, Mr Torrance. How the crew reacts and what orders they are given are down to me."

What on earth were they arguing about?

"That is correct, Captain. However, your judgment is clearly impaired, and the nature of your relationship with Mrs Fisher renders you incapable of making a rational decision in this case. If you will not uphold the order, I will go over your head. There is a missing child and a passenger who may have been murdered. Why are you not taking it seriously?"

I couldn't help myself, I had to peek around the corner.

Alistair's nostrils flared, something they did when he was fighting to control his anger. He was looking down at a shorter man wearing a suit. They were both in the passageway outside my suite where a stand-off was taking place.

Jermaine and Barbie were in the doorway to my suite, and flanking Alistair were Martin, Deepa, Schneider, Sam, and Pippin. Facing off against them, the short man in the suit had half a dozen other securit y officers with him, among whom I could see Nichols and Harvey. The man in the suit looked to have enlisted their help. I had no idea who he was, but he clearly held some sway in an official capacity.

I ducked my head back out of sight and continued to listen.

Alistair said, "I have already explained that Mrs Fisher is not in her accommodation, Mr Torrance."

"Yes," agreed the short man. "And it concerns me greatly that you either will not tell me or simply do not know her whereabouts."

Alistair continued to argue in the calm manner he almost always maintains.

"Mrs Fisher is not required to tell anyone where she is. Her role as the ship's detective is such that she must, on occasion, assume an undercover identity. This will not be the first time she has vanished only to reappear with a crime solved."

"Yet she stands accused; named by the mother of the missing child immediately before she herself was silenced. Patricia Fisher is wanted for kidnap and under suspicion of murder ..."

My hands flew to my face. This was the little surprise Angelica arranged for me! Another lie, acted out by her or by someone in her employment to ensure that not only could I not get help from my friends, get a shower, charge my phone, or change my outfit, I was going to have enormous difficulty moving around the ship no matter what I was wearing.

"… and your security team is going to quietly tear this ship apart looking for her." Mr Torrance concluded.

I backed away a pace, my head filling with questions. Would I be best served to simply hand myself over? The thought had occurred to me last night as well, but wasn't me behind bars what Angelica wanted? She wanted to see me fall from grace and end up penniless and friendless with my reputation in tatters and nowhere I could go without being recognised and ridiculed.

The two most recent tasks I'd been assigned were going to help to achieve that faster than last night's idiocy. That it was time to fight back went without saying, and to do that I had to be mobile. I would find a way to charge my phone soon enough – it wasn't that much of a challenge, but first I needed to get rid of my shadow.

Backing away from my suite I realised why Angelica had told me I could go there – so she would know precisely where I was and could set someone to follow me around again. I didn't know if the young Asian man I'd seen last night was the only one shadowing me and had no idea if Barbie and the others had any luck finding him from the broad description I sent them on the tissue.

I got my answer a moment later when I spotted him trying to stay just out of sight. Whoever he was, close quarter surveillance was not in his skillset for this was now twice I'd seen him. Last night I lost him by creating bedlam and by going faster than he could hope to match. I could do the same again now, but on my way to tackle the next insane task on Angelica's list, I was going to ambush my shadow instead.

It was still too early in the day for a lot of the ship's passengers to be up, so the decks were sparsely populated as I made my way back around the top deck. I made my movements obvious because I wanted the man to see where I was going, and chose a passageway that would give him a clear view to see me going outside.

A jogger passed me, a muffled tune coming from the earbuds she wore. I turned to go in the opposite direction to the one she was travelling, my route already planned in my head.

The sundeck outside the ship's structure was even emptier than inside – perfect for my intentions, and I moved quickly to get into position.

Confrontation

When the young man cautiously pushed the door open to step out onto the sundeck, I was hidden behind the awning of a bar positioned near the top deck swimming pool. Hidden by the darkness under the awning, I waited until he was five yards away from the doors and well into the open.

He was looking around for me, frantically searching and straining his hearing in the hope he might discover which direction I had gone.

Now that he could not immediately escape me, I stepped out in the daylight. He saw me immediately, my movement catching his eye. Momentarily startled, the man's feet twitched with indecision.

"Why are you doing this?" I asked, striding across the sundeck toward him.

He looked around, checking to see if it was just the two of us. I expected him to relax when he saw that we were alone. He would have the upper hand, but far from it, he began to back away and looked positively terrified of me.

"It was money," he admitted. "I thought it was going to be an easy job. Now I just want to get away. She's completely mad!" he blurted as he bolted for the door to get back inside the ship.

His reaction was about as far from what I expected as possible, but it was also enormously pleasing. Did this mean I was now free from being followed?

The back of my skull itched like mad, and the world slowed for a moment as I analysed my most recent thought. It went back to my call to Angelica. I'd questioned whether there was a bug in the phone she'd given me, but she didn't know where I'd been all night.

Had there been a bug, it would have told her I was trapped in the Hudson Suite. This was both good news and bad. Good because it meant it was possible to avoid being followed, but bad because she had another method by which she was tracking my movements. It wasn't fool proof, but until I figured out what it was, I couldn't risk sneaking off to get help.

The doors to get back inside slammed shut behind the young man and I cursed myself for not reacting more swiftly. I want to claim that I exploded into action. Honestly though, I chased after him as swiftly as I possibly could on my little fifty-three-year-old legs. If he was fed up working for Angelica, he might be willing to give up everything he knew. He could tell me where she was for a start.

I cursed again for not thinking of this sooner.

Bursting through the door to get back inside, I found the passageway to be empty but could hear running footsteps fading into the distance. Sucking in some air, I gave chase.

Not for long though.

I got about ten yards before the inevitable happened. A white uniform stepped into view. This placed an obstacle between me and my quarry, but that was a lesser concern than the look of recognition on the security officer's face.

"Mrs Fisher!" Lieutenant Kashmir exclaimed his surprise.

"I'm innocent," I assured him, braking hard to stop myself before I got within easy grabbing reach.

Lieutenant Kashmir put his hands out to prevent me chasing the young Asian man, not that I had plans to try to force my way past, but he didn't try to get to me.

"I don't doubt it, Mrs Fisher. It might be best though if I take you into custody."

"You can't!" I started backing away again. "You know what's been going on better than most. Heck you were attacked. Wait, why are you even in uniform? You were concussed last night."

Kashmir snorted a laugh and sighed. "Orders. There's a report of a kidnapped child. It came over one of the ship's phones and the woman said it was you who attacked her. She was adamant that Patricia Fisher had attacked her at knifepoint. I heard the recording, Mrs Fisher, it was very convincing. It ended with the woman screaming that you were coming for her. All time off is cancelled until you are found. I have no choice but to take you in."

I backed away again. "Don't you see, this is precisely what Angelica wants. Everyone knows I've been looking for Angelica Howard-Box. She's the one who knocked you out yesterday. She has my dogs and she set up this hoax." I sure hoped it was a hoax and that Angelica hadn't actually kidnapped a kid to frame me. Not that I would put it past her. "If you take me in, who will be looking for her? You must let me go. That man who just ran by you ..."

Kashmir glanced in the direction I was looking.

"What man?" he asked.

I couldn't believe it. "Oh, come on, Berhouz, you must have seen him. Tall, lean, in his twenties, Chinese or Taiwanese maybe. You didn't see h im?"

Lieutenant Kashmir made an apologetic face, but wasn't taking his eyes off me and was starting to creep closer.

"Look," I backed away as he came forward. "I just caught the man who has been tailing me. I have evidence. You can take it to Lieutenant

Commander Baker and the rest of my team. They can catch him and then they can catch Angelica."

Kashmir's expression changed, his focus shifting away from me as he tussled internally with what to do.

To push him over the edge, I said, "You know me, Berhouz. I didn't kidnap a child or hurt anyone. I'm trying to get my dogs back and I'm going to catch Angelica just like I catch everyone else."

They were bold words, but they did the trick.

Lieutenant Kashmir nodded once, slowly. "Okay, Mrs Fisher. I believe you."

I sagged with relief.

"I still have to take you in though. Orders are orders."

My eyes flared with shock – he was reaching for his sidearm. There are no words to describe how startled I felt. Yesterday he was looking after my dogs, now he was about to point a gun at me.

A gasp of air filled my lungs as I twisted around and started to run. Kashmir yelled for me to stop, but I knew he wasn't going to discharge his weapon. It would cost him his job if he did – security officers carry sidearms as a precaution only. They were to be employed only to save lives.

I ran at the doors, burst through them and back out onto the sun deck with a grunt of pain from my leading shoulder.

"Stop, Mrs Fisher!"

Kashmir's cries fell on deaf ears. I needed to run as fast as I could and get out of sight. The area would fill with his colleagues in no time at all.

However, my plan to find stairs, double back, go inside and find an elevator to ride all went south when I heard him call out again.

"Mrs Fisher?"

It was not the demanding shout for me to stop, but a curious wail of worry. Unable to help myself, I twisted at the waist to look behind me.

Lieutenant Kashmir had already given up the chase, his footsteps faltering as he slowed to a stop. One hand was out, looking for something it could brace against as his knees went to jelly.

"Berhouz?" I questioned, my pace slowing to a stop.

He gave me one last look as he landed on his knees, then I got to watch his eyes roll up into his skull. I was already on my way back to him when he keeled over to slump unmoving onto the deck. If this was a ruse, then he was playing it well. I genuinely believed he was unconscious and when I got to him, he made no attempt to grab me.

His pulse was steady, but he didn't react to voice or touch. Wrestling with my options, I grimaced and picked up his radio.

"Officer down. Top deck, starboard side. Forward of the sundeck centre entrance. Lieutenant Kashmir requires urgent medical assistance." I released the send switch, checked his pulse again, and got to my feet.

He was going to be okay, but if I stayed with him, I wouldn't be. I got moving, but two paces later, I went back. With a muttered apology, I took his universal key card – the device that would get me through almost any door on the ship, and his sidearm.

I hate guns. Hate them. I have never fired one and doubt I ever will, but in my current desperate state, if I saw the young Asian man again, I was going to pin him in place until the security team turned up. He wouldn't know that I didn't even know how to work the safety.

Before anyone could arrive to ruin my getaway, I pocketed the gun in my handbag and left Kashmir where he was. Did I feel bad about it? Yes, very much so. It wasn't me doing it though, it was Angelica.

Hurrying away, I checked the time on the burner phone. It had been nearly half an hour since Angelica gave me my latest silly tasks and I needed to get on with them.

Exit Strategy

Jordan collapsed against a bulkhead and gasped for air. Very little about this job had been what he expected, but it had gone from bad to worse and now he was scared for his life.

The decision to escape Angelica came days ago, but when they started searching the ship for her, and she moved into his cabin, his chance to sneak away evaporated. He should have left in Lanzarote, but having failed to do so because Angelica had just given him an extra ten grand to help her break into Patricia Fisher's suite, he missed his chance.

The next opportunity was going to be in Rio, but he needed his passport for that, and he was certain Angelica had it. The ship was going to arrive at the Brazilian port tomorrow, leaving him less than thirty-six hours to enact 'the plan'. He'd been thinking about it ever since Angelica left him alone with her computer.

"Never trust a hacker," he'd chuckled to himself as he broke through her simplistic password and copied all her files.

With or without his passport, he was getting off the ship the first chance he got. That decision was made before they reached the British Union Isles and cemented without option for reconsideration five minutes ago when he fled from Patricia Fisher.

He wasn't cut out for this kind of work. He was a hacker. He committed crime using a computer while wearing pyjamas and eating a bowl of fruit loops. That's where he was comfortable.

Patricia Fisher knew what he looked like and that was going to get him caught. The only course of action Jordan could see, beyond enacting 'the plan', was to hide. He would grab his emergency pack of possessions; carefully taken from the cabin over the course of the last few days, and stay out of sight until the ship docked.

If he didn't, Angelica would send her tame security officer after him and Jordan knew what that meant. Jordan had listened when she convinced the treacherous security guard that he needed to get closer to Mrs Fisher. He had to make sure she trusted him so he could report back on her movements and what she had discovered. He'd achieved it too, positioning himself close to the English sleuth over the last few weeks. He was trusted, and often seen in her company.

If Angelica ordered it, Jordan felt certain the man would kill him without giving it a second thought. Well, he was out. All he needed was his bag of things and a connection to the internet. He would change the passenger manifest again, concoct a story about being robbed of his wallet and passport, and find a way to get off the ship.

As for Angelica ... he doubted she would even see his parting manoeuvre coming.

Itsy Bitsy Teeny Weeny

One thing I was certain of was the need to change my appearance. The young Asian man might be off my tail, but I was certain Angelica had another method for tracking my movements. Was it another person I was yet to spot, or was it something more sophisticated?

It wouldn't matter either way if I didn't ditch the pink kitten outfit soon. The security team was looking for me and I was easy to spot. Moving swiftly, I had a destination in mind. Now I just needed to get there.

However, where I was going was not the foremost thought in my head.

When Angelica sent me the picture of my dogs, she hadn't given sufficient thought to how well I know the ship. In the background behind

Anna and Georgie, I could see the décor on the walls and though Angelica probably didn't know it, each deck is decorated differently.

She was on the eighth deck, the certain knowledge narrowing my search instantly. Okay, so there were like a thousand cabins on deck eight, but I was able to narrow it down a little further yet. The wall behind the dogs showed no porthole which meant it wasn't one of the cabins on the outer ring. That reduced the search by about twenty percent, and the configuration of the bedroom was that of a standard economy plus cabin, which took the number of cabins she could be in down to about two hundred.

That was still too many and it proved how savvy she was to cut me off from my team, because with them I would find her in minutes.

My phone had died and that made getting some juice into it my top priority. That and finding new clothes. Were it not for all the security guards out looking for me and the likelihood that the rest of the crew was alerted to report seeing me, I would have taken myself to a boutique and bought a new outfit. Even attempting it would get me caught, but knowing the ship as I do, I went to the pool.

One of the pools anyway.

On deck seventeen at the stern of the ship, sits a wave pool where people can surf. Sort of. The permanent wave, with water jetting over a curved surface, allows the athletic instructors to demonstrate how 'easy' it is to the excited passengers who want to give it a go.

I went on once, promptly fell off, got shot across the 'pool' and ended up with my bum in the air and my head under water until one of the lifeguards rescued me.

I wasn't about to try it again, but I was going to find a change of clothes in the locker room. As the name suggests, people's clothes went into lockers, but the lockers were tiny, so anyone bringing a bag along found they had to take it to the wave pool with them or dump it on top of the lockers.

Hoping I would find the ladies' locker room empty and a selection of bags to pick from, I was disappointed to discover there was only one. My pulse hammered in my head as I rifled through another person's belongings, but I found a swimsuit ... okay, a bikini.

It was far too revealing for me, the top part little more than two triangles and some string, but I saw few choices and knew I could make the outfit work. I stole the bikini and risked an extra couple of minutes so I could get a shower.

Taking two towels from the pile available, I wrapped one around my hair, hiding the shocking pink from sight, and another around my body for modesty. Anyone looking for a madwoman in a pink anime kitten outfit wouldn't give me a second glance. Anyone looking for Patricia Fisher, however, was going to see my face.

The cat whiskers had washed off, which was a relief, but looking in the mirror for the first time since I left the salon last night, I could now see the bruising around my left eye and the damage to my lip. I curled it over, inspecting the inside where it was split and angry. Both would heal and I dismissed them as insignificant.

To hide my face I needed a mask, and I found one in the form of factor fifty sun block. There was a stick of it in the same bag where I found the bikini, the coloured kind that you see cricketers use sometimes if they are going to be out in the sun for hours.

In a jiffy, my face was coloured a light, lime green shade.

It was the best I could do. The daft outfit from last night got shoved unceremoniously into a locker and I vowed to never come back for it. Now I could hope to make it to the next task without getting caught.

My friends would be working to clear my name and prove the kid-nap/murder story was bogus and they would still be trying to find the young Asian man I'd unsuccessfully chased. I could narrow down the search area to find Angelica, but that didn't do me any good unless I could tell someone about it. For the life of me, I still couldn't remember anyone's number, so I was just as alone as I had been since the start.

With time ticking away, there was no option but to carry on with the next task on Angelica's insane list. I was going to rob someone.

Angelica wanted me to steal a necklace. A diamond solitaire. She gave me a cabin number and left me to figure out the rest of the details.

Burglary not Theft

Picking a route had been hard because the day was progressing, and passengers were filling the more popular areas. This gave me people among whom I could hide, but also a great concentration of crew, any of whom might question why a woman had gone to such lengths to cover her face in sun block. The alternative was to stick to the less frequented areas, but there, if I came across a security officer, the likelihood of being identified was much higher.

Despite my stomach-clenching worry, I made it from A to B without attracting so much as a passing glance from any of the security I saw.

Now staring at the door to cabin 1878, I questioned who was staying in it. It could be anyone. On the eighteenth deck, it was one of the pricier standard cabins, but it wasn't a suite. The residents were unlikely to be anyone rich or famous, but Angelica had directed me to target this cabin specifically.

Why?

There had to be a reason. It put me on edge that I had no idea what it could be. Was the necklace I was supposed to find some priceless heirloom my adversary somehow knew about?

Swiping Kashmir's universal key card against the lock, I opened it a crack and called out, "Cleaning." Pretending I was there to clean the room, even though I knew the cleaning crews wouldn't get started for another hour, I listened, called again, and slipped inside.

Leaning against the door now that it was closed and I could breathe a temporary sigh of relief, I closed my eyes for a moment and asked what the heck I was doing.

There were a couple of reasons why I was willing to go along with this task other than the obvious one: Angelica would kill Anna and Georgie if I didn't.

Firstly, if I was inside a cabin, I was out of sight. Getting from the wave pool to my current location had taken me close to more than a dozen members of the ship's security team. They all knew me, and in theory might listen. Kashmir hadn't though, and had he not collapsed, he would have caught me.

Secondly, I could find a proper change of clothes and, with luck, a charger for my phone.

Not only that, I could commit the crime, but leave a note explaining why and who I was. I wasn't going to keep the necklace Angelica insisted I had to steal, so yes, she could make me look bad, but I could make it clear my actions were under duress. When the dust settled, the victim of my burglary would understand, I felt certain.

Snapping my eyes open and pushing away from the door, I set about the despicable deed. On the dressing table next to the bed – even on the eighteenth deck the cabins only had one room plus a bathroom so I could see everything straight away – I found a charger. Relieved, I plugged it into my phone.

I waited a few seconds, telling myself the residents of cabin 1878 were probably gone for the day, and moved away only when the screen on my phone came back to life. There were no messages waiting to be read and none pinged into existence now that it was alive again and could receive them.

Next, because I was at the dressing table, I started opening drawers, looking for the necklace. Angelica described it as a diamond solitaire encrusted with emeralds. I didn't find it, but starkly I didn't find any jewellery at all. Not even a pair of earrings.

Now questioning if I might be in a man's room, or that of a gay couple, I moved to the wardrobe. My question was answered by the sight of ladies' apparel. A rack of cocktail dresses hung above stiletto heels, telling me the lady had taste, and ... big feet. I almost picked up one shoe so curious was I by the girth and length of the foot that had to go in it. I wanted to see what size was listed in the shoe, but I stopped myself – it was hardly a priority.

What I needed to do was write the note. If the passengers returned to their cabin and caught me here, it would be easier to explain if the confession explaining my predicament was already there for them.

The writing set – a standard inclusion in every cabin – included embossed paper along with envelopes, and Aurelia postcards. I selected a sheet of paper and scribbled as legibly as possible while also writing more quickly than I normally would.

Letter finished, I pushed back from the desk and scratched my chin. What would Angelica say if I claimed to have gone to the cabin as instructed, but couldn't find the necklace? Should I call her and find out?

Like a light coming on, my brain supplied the answer: there was no necklace and never had been. I was expected to get caught here, rifling through another person's cabin. On top of the bogus kidnapping/murder claim it wouldn't matter what story I told them and whether it was true or not. The pink hair would be sufficient to convince them I was the same person who stole the kid's scooter last night – I was certain they were still following that one up, and the case against me would be enough to do precisely what Angelica wanted. There would be a scandal. My name would appear in the paper as passengers sold their story, and the cruise line would wash their hands of me.

I would escape jail, obviously, but Angelica would do enough damage.

I had to get out and I had to go now. I took two paces and changed my mind. I was still wearing a micro bikini and towels. It was hardly the best outfit for doing … anything. Taking someone else's clothes wasn't something I wanted to do, but telling myself I would do my utmost to reimburse them, I went to the chest of drawers and hoped I would find something that would fit me. I needed a hat too, something that would cover my hair, or a wig; I reflected on some of the disguises I'd worn in the past. It had all been so easy when I had people to help me.

There were sweatpants in the drawer and t-shirts, the kind that are supposed to cling to your skin and most women my age avoid.

It was going to have to do. I shucked the towels, and it was at that precise second that I heard the lock operate. Someone outside had just swiped their key card and they were coming in. The door was starting to move inward, and I got to hear the voices of the people outside.

They were South African, not that it mattered, because they were coming in and I was trapped.

I ran, yanking my phone from the charger cable and throwing myself into the cabin's bathroom where, out of sight, I froze.

The couple stopped talking mid-sentence. Had they seen the note, the towels on the floor, or the open drawers? It didn't exactly matter which clue had given me away – I was trapped yet again either way.

"Someone's been in here," observed the women.

"You think so, Laney? What gave you the first hint?" the man replied snarkily.

Tutting, Laney replied, "There's no need to be unpleasant, Greg. Check the bathroom and see if there's anyone in there."

I had no desire to be caught cowering in a bathroom, and figured I stood a better chance of talking my way out of it if I came clean and asked for their help. Stepping out from behind the door with my hands held at shoulder height in surrender, the words I planned to say caught in my mouth when I saw the cabin's residents.

Their appearance was such a shock to me, I almost choked.

The man was more muscular than any person I had ever seen and the woman a yard behind him was no slouch either. They had to have just come from the gym as they were both bathed in sweat and the veins running over their exposed skin, of which there was plenty, were standing out like rivers on a map. Both, in their early thirties and well over six feet tall, looked like they could crush cars without the need for machinery or tools.

Greg, standing just a few feet from me, let his eyes rove up and down my body in a leering manner that made me feel even more naked than the micro bikini.

"You got me a gift," he gasped. "Babe, thank you. It's not even my birthday."

I blinked, certain I understood his meaning, but questioning it, nevertheless.

"Excuse me? A gift?" I mumbled.

Greg's smile, which had been beaming, had sort of frozen and was starting to fade as he continued to stare at me.

Over his shoulder, he asked, "Couldn't you have found someone a little younger?"

Unable to believe my ears, I blurted, "Excuse me!"

Laney's face wasn't smiling. Her face was a thunder cloud of anger, and it was aimed at me.

"She's not a gift, Greg. She's a thief. She broke in here to rob us."

"No, I didn't. I'm ..."

Greg shouted, "Shut up!" The ferocity of it silencing me instantly.

Leering at me, he snarled, "I'm gonna tear off your arms and beat you to death with them." As threats go it was right up there in my all-time top ten.

I almost wet myself and gripped by terror I darted backwards into the bathroom once more and threw the door shut, locking it with a flick.

"I need your help!" I squealed through the door. "I wasn't trying to rob you. I'm in trouble."

"Yeah, you are," sniggered Greg from behind the door. Then, in a sing song voice, he taunted, "Little pig, little pig, let me in."

'Not by the hair of my chinny-chin-chin' came to mind as a potential reply though I dismissed it and got no time to think of anything better to say because the door proved to be no obstacle at all. Greg punched straight through it with a single blow.

Angelica had sent me to the cabin because she wanted to get me beaten up. My best guess was that one of her assistants had spotted the steroid abusing couple and knew their routine. She intended for me to get caught by them and either beaten up, which looked likely to happen, or held in their cabin unable to escape until security arrived.

With all the other charges against me, this would be the icing on the cake. Especially since I had just left Kashmir in an injured state and taken his sidearm.

His sidearm! It was in my handbag on the carpet by the desk.

The wood in the frame splintered, pieces flying off to land in the bath and the door swung back to crash into the toilet where there wasn't enough room for it to complete the full arc. Now, the hole that once contained the door was filled with the girth of Greg's shoulders.

"Time to die, robber," he taunted, his meaty hands opening and closing.

My eyes were wide with a terror so complete I couldn't get my feet to work, but I managed to mumble, "It would be burglary."

He hesitated. "What?"

"Burglary," I attempted to clarify. "You called me a robber, but the crime of robbery involves violence."

"Oh, this is going to involve violence, lady." Greg took a step forward and I think he might have beaten me half to death in the next few seconds had Laney not grabbed him from behind.

"You'll get blood everywhere, dummy. Why is it that you always think extreme violence is the answer?"

Greg pulled a face that mocked his partner for asking the question.

"Oh, I don't know. Because I'm a mixed martial arts cage fighting champion?"

Laney rolled her eyes. "So am I, Greg. It doesn't mean I feel the need to brutally bludgeon everyone I ever meet. You can knock her out and throw her overboard."

"What!" I couldn't believe my ears. They believed I had broken into their cabin, and I understood their lack of trust, but they were talking about killing me.

Greg took a step toward me, and I sucked in a deep breath to fuel the scream I was about to emit. His giant, meaty hand shot out to clamp over my mouth.

"Just don't do it yet," Laney cautioned. "We need to check the stash first, and we need to be sure she's working alone."

Using his other hand to grab my head, Greg pulled me from the bathroom and into the cabin where he threw me at the bed.

Though my head was filled with words I wanted to use to convince the couple I was neither threat nor thief, I had fallen silent because Laney had used the word 'stash'. The way she employed it could only mean they were up to no good.

"Don't move," Greg threatened, a pudgy digit pointing my way like a threat.

Right before my eyes Laney removed the bottom drawer from their chest of drawers and from beneath it extracted a leather briefcase. Snap, snap, went the clasps as they popped open and all the guesses I'd made in the last few seconds – drugs, forged documents, dodgy pharmaceuticals, cash – were all wrong. The briefcase contained a moulded liner in which sat row upon row of casino chips.

Had I seen them in different circumstances, I might have assumed the couple had won big, but these were Aurelia casino chips and each of them was a ten thousand. I had to be looking at about five million in chips. Except almost a whole row was missing. The notion of a discrepancy in the casino takings – the number failing to tally – had reached my ears days ago, but no one had yet suggested it was anything but a bookkeeping error. Clearly that was not the case.

Greg, waiting impatiently, said, "Well?"

Laney inhaled deeply through her nose before saying, "They are all there. So is the cash," she added, lifting a bag filled with bundles of notes.

"Do you think we ought to call, Roger," asked Greg.

Laney twisted around to look up at him.

"What for?"

Greg made an exasperated noise, like he shouldn't have to explain because it was obvious.

"Because she knew to come to our cabin."

They were talking back and forth and paying little attention to me. It gave me a chance to look around. The only way out was the door that led to the passageway outside. If I heard someone walking by, I could scream for help.

Assuming I was heard, it wouldn't result in my immediate rescue. The person outside wouldn't smash down the door. However, they might call security and at this point I would be relieved to see their white uniforms. Unfortunately, I wasn't hearing any footsteps.

My handbag was where I'd left it – on the carpet next to the desk, but to get to it, I would need to get around Greg. I did not like my chances and I wasn't happy with the concept of brandishing a firearm anyway.

Would I do it to save my life? Yes. However, since I couldn't get to it, the answer was moot.

Laney, conceding to Greg's point about contacting Roger – whoever that was, had placed the chips and cash back under the bottom drawer and was getting to her feet.

"I'll call him," she remarked, taking a phone from a pocket on the hip of her stretchy sports pants. She was facing the desk and I saw when she clocked the note I'd left there for her to find. She glanced at Greg when she picked it up. "What's this?"

She wasn't expecting an answer and didn't get one for Greg could see she was already reading it, her eyes skipping over the lines.

With neither one watching me, I had moved to the edge of the bed. The way I saw it I had two routes by which I might try to get away. I could try to get to the door which would give me access to the rest of the ship and the chance to run away screaming for help. My alternative was the balcony that came with the level of cabin they'd chosen. I'd noticed the sliding door was just slightly ajar so I knew it wasn't locked. Getting to it would take me away from the potentially murderous couple, but what then?

If I made it to the balcony, to escape I would have to jump across the gap to the next cabin along – an improbable feat - or drop to the one below – a feat which while more achievable guaranteed death if I missed, slipped, or lost my grip.

The choices I had were stomach-clenchingly terrifying and there were still no sounds from the passageway outside.

Laney employed a small handbook's worth of curse words as she got to the good bit of the letter and swung her head and eyes up to gawp at me.

"What?" demanded Greg, following her gaze so they were both staring at me. "What is it?"

Laney's cheeks were flushed red, heat rising from them as adrenalin gripped her.

She nodded her head in my direction. "That's Patricia Fisher. Remember I told you about that English lady who broke up the organised crime family? That's her." Laney jabbed a finger at me. "She's some kind of super sleuth and she broke into our cabin. She knows about the scam, Greg. She must do."

Fear shot through Greg's eyes, the emotion looking out of place on the hulking brute's face.

"Izzat so? Then I guess we don't have much choice about what we do next."

Tapping Greg on the arm, she said, "Just keep her there while I call Roger."

I didn't dare move for fear Greg might claim I was trying to escape and use force to stop me. However, having seen how nervous they were now, a third avenue of escape occurred to me.

"That's right," I announced with bold confidence, interrupting Laney before she could make her call. "I needed you to identify the third person, the one who works in the casino. Thank you for that." Okay, so I was guessing Roger worked in the casino, but figuring things out in my head, I couldn't see how else their scam could work. They would need someone on the inside. "Of course, this whole episode is being recorded," I lied.

Greg and Laney looked deeply worried now, their eyes filling with panic as the colour drained from their cheeks.

"There really isn't anywhere to run. Members of ship's security are waiting for my signal to swoop."

"What happens if you don't give the signal?" asked Laney, spotting a hole in my hastily concocted plan. Clearly, the brains of the outfit, she nudged Greg. "Don't let her move. I'm going to call Roger and find out if she is bluffing."

Thinking as fast as my brain would work, I couldn't come up with anything I could do or say to improve my situation. Laney was talking to Roger on her phone, confirming in seconds that he was a member of the crew when he told her everyone on the ship was after me. He was coming to them, his advice regarding me only that they needed to make me disappear.

Ending the call, Laney told Greg, "It looks like we are in the clear. She's on her own. Seems she's wanted for something she's done. Get her bag. We'll dump it and her over the side. Bye bye sleuth, bye bye recorded confession."

Greg's face split into an evil grin and he scooped my handbag with one hand.

Though it terrified me to do so, and I was shocked that I even did it, I darted forward to jam my right hand inside the bag as he held it up. They had both chosen to peer inside, curiosity getting the better of them, so they failed to notice that I was moving until it was too late.

It was what Barbie would refer to as a 'Hail Mary' play. Though I wasn't sure where the name came from and believed it was most commonly used as a sporting term, it suited what I was doing because I either got this right or they were going to kill me.

My fingers found the gun and I yanked it from my handbag and pointed it at them as I backed away.

Sensing something was wrong, I looked down at my hands to find I had the gun around the wrong way. I was holding the muzzle with the handle pointing at them. With a squeal of panic, I reversed my grip and got it pointing the right way.

"Back up," I commanded, trying really hard to make it sound like I wasn't ready to wet myself. My hands were shaking and consequently so was the gun.

Greg snorted a laugh and I shot him.

I didn't mean to. Honest. I expected the safety to be on and I think my eyes were closed when the trigger gave way far more easily than I expected.

The shot passed through the groin of his baggy sweatpants, exiting on the other side where I heard the bullet bury itself in the deck by the door.

I squealed in surprise, Laney screamed with fright, and Greg fainted.

There was never going to be a better chance than this, so even though I was ready to throw up or pass out, whichever came first, I grabbed the handbag – dropped by Greg's feet when he flopped to the carpet - and ran to the door.

"You shot him!" squealed Laney. "You shot him in the pants! If you've shot his junk off …"

I've never been a fan of the younger generation's desire to refer to their intimate body parts as junk, but this wasn't the time to discuss it. Hurrying to the door, my gun still trained roughly in Laney's direction though it was shaking more than ever, I had a parting comment.

"I'll be coming back for you as soon as I have cleared my name. Your best bet is to turn yourself in."

I doubted she would do any such thing, but the moment I got into the passageway outside, there were footsteps coming my way, the distinctive sound of the ship's security team. Reacting to reports of a shot fired, no doubt, they ran by me when I ducked into an alcove.

Just as they ran by and I breathed a sigh of relief, the phone rang in my bag, its sudden unexpectedness making my heart skip a beat. I sagged against a wall, praying the day would come to a stop, but knowing it had to be Angelica, I pulled it from my bag and pressed the green button.

Tactical Threats

"Well, I must say I am surprised to see you in one piece, Patricia. I'm a little disappointed and at the same time forced to admit that I am impressed."

"Gee, that makes me feel so much better about my day," I was full of sarcasm.

"Now, now, Patricia. I'll thank you to remain polite."

I ignored her remark and posed a question that I knew she wouldn't answer.

"How do you know I got out in one piece?"

Her reply carried her usual superior tone plus a trace of amusement.

"Wouldn't you like to know."

Yes, I would. "I met your spy," I let her know, curious to hear how she might react. "The young Asian man? I wonder, was he the one who hacked my computer and cloned my emails? He had that look about him – intelligent yet shifty." Angelica didn't respond. Was she surprised by the news? I pressed on, "He doesn't like working for you; that was abundantly clear. In fact, he came across as scared of you and called you mad."

Angelica finally snapped, "That is enough, Patricia. Congratulations on completing another task. However, if you are pleased with yourself, remember that you are now guilty of breaking and entering on top of all your other crimes. Your own beloved security team is hunting for you, Patricia. How does that feel?"

I laughed at her and it was genuine amusement I felt.

"How does it feel? Like most other days, if I am being honest. No one has shot at me so far, so all things considered, I'm doing quite well. Tell me Angelica, do you really think you can win? How do you expect to get off the ship when all this is over? You are going to get caught, Angelica. Is that what you want? You'll end up behind bars? What will Bobbie think of that?" My decision to employ her son's name was tactical – I needed to confirm she would react as I expected.

"How dare you speak his name! You ruined his life! You destroyed his marriage before he could even say his vows!"

"I believe you mean I allowed him to admit the truth and be with the woman he loved, rather than the one you picked for him." It was another taunt, a jab with a sharp stick into an already open wound.

Angelica raged like a beast, "Which dog, Patricia? Which dog goes for a swim first? Pick one! I'm opening the porthole right now."

It was a terrifying demand that made me feel faint and sick at the same time. However, though my heart told me I was gambling with my dogs' lives, my head knew differently. Angelica didn't have a porthole and far more than she wanted to punish me by harming my dogs, she wanted to ruin my reputation and witness all the damage she could inflict.

Carefully, respectfully, I threatened her. "If you harm either one of my dogs, Angelica. If I even suspect that you have, I will end this ridiculous charade, hand myself in, and make sure every security officer on this ship is actively engaged in finding you. You want to see me fall from grace? Well, the only way that is going to happen is if you keep me in play. I will perform your next stupid task, undoubtedly creating more trouble for me to try to talk my way out of later. And maybe you will win, and I will find myself back in England with nothing but shocking headlines to follow me. But not if you hurt my dogs. I want another photograph of them, Angelica. Send it now and tell me what you want me to do next. I will jump through your hoops for as long as I can stay ahead of the ship's security team ... please tell me there isn't actually a missing child somewhere on this ship." I had always doubted Angelica would actually hurt anyone, but how sure was I?

"Of course not, Patricia. Of the two of us, only one is capable of such a heinous act."

From a certain standpoint, Angelica's level of delusion was intriguing.

"I will send you the photograph, Patricia, but since you are being rude and arguing, the next task will be one that you won't want to do."

I choked on my laugh. "Really? You have worse tasks lined up for me yet?"

Angelica's deliciously happy reply of, "Oh, yes," should have warned me of what was to come, but because my brain doesn't work in the same twisted manner as hers, the content of the message she sent came as a shock.

Hubba Hubba

Immediately, I sent a text back to her. '*Where am I supposed to get a tattoo, Angelica? There are no tattoo parlours on board the ship.*'

I got a single word response. '*Improvise.*'

"Improvise?" I muttered. I will eternally claim that I am not a violent person and would never want to see anyone in pain. Angelica was pushing my buttons though and I had a gun. It was probably a good thing I didn't know where she was.

Still dressed in a micro bikini that not only felt like it was sawing my backend in half, but would also draw attention now that I no longer had a towel to cover myself, I chose to head for the one place I would get fewer looks: the sun terrace.

There are pools all over the ship, the Aurelia like so many cruise ships, spent a lot of its time in warm climates. A few of the pools are indoors, but most of them are outside where sun worshippers can work on their tan and this close to the equator, I knew for certain there would be very few free sunbeds to be had at any of them.

Leaving cabin 1878 behind, it wasn't far to go to get back outside the ship. To say I felt exposed was about as big of an understatement as I could possibly make, and it went two-fold for it was physical and emotional right now. There was so little material in the bikini I felt utterly on display.

Do I admire the women who can pull off such an outfit? Sort of, I guess, though envy might be a better word. However, even if my figure were such that revealing it was something I wanted to do, I still wouldn't, it's just not in my nature. The sun block shielded the fact that I was blushing crimson red as I made my way to the pool, and I tried hard to ignore the looks I got.

Once there, I made a beeline for the pile of towels, and covered myself again. Mentally breathing a sigh of relief, I decided to chance speaking to a member of crew. I wanted to embellish my outfit. Next to one of the open-air bars was a kiosk selling hats, sarongs, sunglasses, and myriad other items such as goggles for the kids to go swimming.

I picked the biggest pair of sunglasses, the lenses a full two and a half inches across. With them in place, the sunblock looked less like an attempt to hide my face. I stuck a wide-brimmed hat on my head, tugging it down at the front to hide as much of me as possible, then added a sarong and a paperback book.

At the payment point, I tore the tag off the sunglasses rather than remove them, and had the woman working the till beep the sarong and hat without me taking them off.

"Do you want a bag for your items?" she asked.

I needed to answer, but would she question my voice when I replied in my usual English accent? How much had the crew been briefed? How well did the woman know Patricia Fisher? I didn't recognise her, but that was a whole different thing. Unfortunately.

Employing what was probably a terrible South African accent because that was what I had just been listening to, I mumbled, "No, thank you," tapped my card against the reader and did not wait for my receipt.

I was trying to act casual and failing miserably.

However, even though the sarong was see-through, I felt distinctly more covered than I had a moment ago. Using the paperback as a shield, I started to look around. I needed someone with a fresh tattoo.

I'd seen them before – people who had chosen to get 'inked' while they were abroad. The whole idea of a tattoo was an odd one to me because it felt like picking a pair of curtains or wallpaper that you were going to have for the rest of your life.

Now was not the time to question it. Angelica had given me specific instructions on what she expected – a tattoo no smaller than two inches in diameter and it had to be on one of my forearms. She wanted, of course, to make sure it would be seen. With a tattoo, which had to clearly say 'fraud' in bold letters, on my arm, I would never again be able to wear short sleeves.

Or I would have to cover it up with an even bigger tattoo.

Resigned to the task, I continued to scan around until I spotted a man in his early thirties. His entire right arm was covered in tattoos, plus he had more across his back and down his legs. One was wrapped tightly with cling film – at least that's what it looked like. I'm no expert, but whatever it is they use, I knew it meant the ink was no more than a day or two old.

He looked up when my shadow fell over him. He'd been ogling a pair of ladies on the other side of the pool, their bikinis almost as revealing as mine.

Tapping his leg to make him move it, I said, "Budge up," and then sat down on the edge of his sun lounger. "I want a tattoo," I announced my purpose for intruding upon his day before he could question me.

"No, you don't," he replied knowingly.

"Yes, I really do." I didn't.

He continued to argue, "I don't think so."

Changing tack, I said, "I'm Patricia."

"Sorry, lady. Not interested."

Unsure what he meant, I tried again. "I'm just looking to ask you a couple of questions about your tattoos," I explained. "Do you know anyone who owns a tattoo gun?" I knew that in theory one could create a tattoo with a ball point pen and a needle, but the thought of trying to do that to myself made me want to vomit. Theoretically, I could stomach someone using a sterilised piece of equipment specifically made for the job.

He sniggered. "That is literally the worst pick up line ever. Did you get help, or did you come up with that by yourself?"

Now feeling offended, I narrowed my eyes at him – not that he could see it behind my sunglasses.

"I am not trying to pick you up. I asked about your tattoos."

He laughed again. "Yeah, right. That's why you came over. You want me to take you back to my cabin so I can "tattoo" you." He put air quotes around the word 'tattoo'. "You want me to tattoo you until you scream my name, right." He winked at me, then cupped one hand to his mouth and shouted, "Predator alert!"

I was horrified. He thought I was after him for sex!

"How old are you, anyway?" he asked, stunning me with his brash cheek. "Maybe try someone a little closer to your own age."

People were looking my way and that was the opposite of what I wanted to achieve. Mumbling to the frowning faces around me as I got up, I assured them it was nothing more than a misunderstanding.

Hurrying away, I headed for the other side of the pool and the back rows of sun loungers. It was far enough away that the people there wouldn't have seen or heard the previous incident. Forcing myself to calm, I found another likely target.

Covered, literally head to toe in tattoos, he was older than me. Much older, I decided as I got closer. He was in his late seventies, though the tattoos, which ran right up his neck to stop just under his chin, distorted the wrinkles his skin had developed and made him look far younger.

I waved as I approached to get his attention.

"Hello," I made my salutation sound innocent and open.

The man looked up, caught sight of me, sat bolt upright on his bed, and said, "Hubba, hubba." To my absolute horror, he then patted his groin and spoke to it. "Wake up! I told you this trip would be worth the money. We've only been on the ship a day and there's a live one on the hook already."

Scarcely able to believe my ears or eyes, I mumbled, "Sorry, I thought you were someone else," and hurried on my way.

I got about five yards before my path was blocked by two young ladies. Both in their twenties, they were heavily tattooed with multiple piercings and a lot of black makeup. One had her arm looped through the other's to suggest they were a couple, and they were clearly in my way on purpose.

Now frantically glancing about and wondering which way I should go, I was hemmed in by the rows of sun loungers. I did not want to go back past Mr Hubba Hubba, but one of the ladies spoke, making me an offer I hadn't expected.

"We can tattoo you," said the one on the right. "If that's what you really want." She was wearing a black bikini and I could see where her nipple piercings distorted the fabric. The left side of her head was shaved, and the rest of her hair swept right over her skull to cascade down the other side. It was dyed black with blond roots just showing through and the final inch or so was deep red. "I'm Tasha," she introduced herself. "This is Roxy."

Roxy waved a hand. "We overheard you talking to that idiot by the pool. We have a tattoo kit in our cabin."

"Like I said," added Tasha, "If that's what you really want."

I both did and I didn't. It wasn't my choice, but there was no need to burden the ladies with my problems, so I nodded gratefully.

"That's very generous of you. Can you do it now?"

Tasha leaned her head back to check with Roxy, who nodded, and it proved to be that easy. I had two ladies who had a tattoo gun in their cabin, and they were prepared to do the deed. I knew next to nothing about tattoos but what I did know was that you can get an outline and then fill in the rest of it later. That was my request.

In my head, it would be easy to get it covered up with something else, if it was just lines and not big blocks of colour. People would ask me about it when I finally decided on a design to cover up the original tattoo, and I would think of something to tell them.

If nothing else, I would be able to claim I had lived an interesting and varied life.

However, the sureness with which I approached the task and the confidence I felt diminished the moment Tasha switched on the machine to test it and I first heard the buzzing noise it made.

"This isn't going to hurt, is it?" I asked, trepidation in my voice.

Roxy sniggered. "Yeah, it is. Forearms are not a great place to get a tattoo. There's not enough fat underneath to absorb it."

"You'd be better off with a deltoid," Tasha commented, tapping her upper left arm to emphasise where she meant.

"Or a thigh," said Roxy. "When I had this one done," she showed me what looked to be a female Samurai warrior in scanty armour and fishnets, holding a sword in one hand and a man's severed head in the other, "I hardly felt a thing."

Good to know, but Angelica wanted me to have one on my forearm. I could do it. I just had to be brave.

"How about some gin?" I asked.

Cuffed

I opened an eye, confusion reigning for a moment as I fought to get my bearings and recall what had happened. For a very brief second, a wave of relief swept over me – it had all been a dream. The whole episode with my dogs going missing and everything that followed was nothing more than one of those terrible nightmares that you cannot wake from and feel utterly convinced are true. That feeling ended when I tried to lift my right hand to my face and the cuffs stopped it.

Restrained by something solid, I twisted my body and jerked from prone to upright in a single move. The sheet covering me fell away, showing me the stupid micro bikini as a flood of terrible memories washed over me.

Tasha and Roxy had given me gin and were surprised when I sank three large ones on the trot like I was doing shots. I had been trying to calm my nerves, but that didn't work because I passed out the moment the needle touched my skin. Jolting again, I pulled back the sheet to look down at my right forearm. There was a tiny blob of angry skin with a miniscule blue mark beneath it. At least they didn't finish the job while I was unconscious.

My best guess was that they called for help, the medics arriving to assess me saw who I was and called security.

I wasn't in the brig though, I was in the sickbay, but I wasn't alone. I was being watched over by Lieutenants Harvey and Nichols – just my luck. They were drinking coffee in the sickbay's small reception area, but seeing I was now awake, the pair were heading my way.

I tugged my right arm, rattling the cuff. "Is this necessary?"

Both men met me with expressionless stares. "Given the list of crimes under your belt today, Mrs Fisher, you're lucky it's not both arms and both ankles," sneered Harvey.

Thankfully, they were not the only people in sick bay. Drs Nakamura and Davis were in attendance and were not about to have their patient bullied.

"Go back and wait by the door, gentlemen," insisted Dr Davis. "The only reason Mrs Fisher is cuffed at all is because she arrived like that, and you have refused to release her."

"Orders," replied Harvey, his tone insubordinate.

Hideki came to my side. "Are you all right, Patricia? Barbie is on her way along with the captain, Jermaine, and your security team. They have all been worried sick about you."

It was a relief to hear I would see my friends soon, but how long had I been out of it? It couldn't have been long, I felt sure, but what had Angelica done in the meantime? Did she know the security team had taken me away?

The sound of approaching voices in the passageway outside soon became the recognisable sound of my friends and my boyfriend, all of whom I was equally pleased to see. They came through the door in a rush, Alistair leading the way.

He rushed over to me. "Patricia."

Jermaine was right behind him, pushing Barbie in her wheelchair, and I saw Sam, Martin, and all the others as they fanned out to surround m e.

"Patty," squealed Barbie, her excitement fading quickly when she got a proper look at me. "Oh, my goodness, what happened?" she asked.

Alistair had come to kiss me, but seeing the fat lip and bruising around my eye, he veered his lips sideways to gently place them on the uninjured side of my face.

"My, darling, are you injured?" he whispered softly.

Jermaine came to my side, not wanting to crowd me, but silently keen to make sure I was okay. I felt infinitely better now that my friends were by my side, but there wasn't much time for conversation.

No one was saying much, each keeping their thoughts as they wondered what awfulness I might have endured to leave me looking as I did.

That is until Sam poked his head between Schneider and Pippin.

"Wow, Mrs Fisher. You've got pink hair! You look like a lollipop!"

I snorted a laugh that burst from my lips and refused to be quashed. Maybe it was tension breaking through the barrier I'd walled it behind or something, but I was laughing now, and I couldn't stop.

It proved to be infectious, my friends and even Alistair joining in with my mirth. It came to an abrupt end when I tried to lift my right hand to wipe the tears from my face.

Spinning around to face Harvey and Nichols, Alistair demanded, "Why is Mrs Fisher in cuffs?"

"Because that is my order, Captain," said the short man I knew as Mr Torrance as he came through the doors to sickbay too. "A better question might be why do you wish to release her?"

The question had been directed at Alistair, but I was the one who answered.

"Because he is wise enough to know that I am innocent of the foolish charges levied against me and is not accustomed to wasting my time, his time, or that of anyone else by pursuing bogus allegations. There is no missing child. The report was made by Angelica Howard-Box and intended to make you dance to her tune. That it worked so effectively is shameful."

It was time for me to defend myself and it was time to get the team working. I knew roughly where Angelica was, and now that I was back with my friends and there was nothing Angelica could do about it, it was time to close the net and catch her. First, I had to get rid of Mr Torrance, but he was already arguing.

"I have a credible report that you discharged a firearm less than an hour ago, Mrs Fisher. This was a firearm you took from the unconscious form of Lieutenant Kashmir after you knocked him out. That's two crimes which alone would see you locked in the brig until we make port and can remove you from the ship. I can add to that the reports from last night - that of a woman matching your description stealing a child's scooter, attempting to rob a steward, fleeing from security, and in general creating more mayhem than I have ever heard of aboard one of Purple Star's ships. I am led to believe you were involved in a sordid sex party of some kind if eyewitness reports are to be believed."

I opened my mouth to retort, but Mr Torrance raised his voice.

"I'm not finished! There is the small fact that the bullet you fired was inside a cabin on the eighteenth deck, was aimed at one of the passengers staying in that cabin, a cabin that you illegally entered." He paused to remove a piece of paper from an inside pocket on his jacket. It was the note I wrote and left for the passengers to find. "I have here a confession," he gloated proudly.

"Yes," I agreed. "What else does it say?"

"I hardly think that matters," he remarked, folding the note and putting it away again.

"Oh, but it really does, Mr Torrance, as does the small fact," I chose to copy his choice of words, "that the couple in question are the ones running the casino scam."

All eyes turned my way, giving me their full attention. Mr Torrance had nothing to say, so I continued.

"They are working with a man from the crew with the first name, Roger. He is their man on the inside. In their cabin beneath their chest of drawers they have a brief case filled with ten-thousand-dollar poker chips. I suspect these to be clever fakes which one of the croupiers is cashing in for them. Are you aware, Mr Torrance, that there is a discrepancy showing in the casino takings?"

"I am aware." He wasn't happy.

"For the last almost twenty-four hours, I have been on the run around the ship while a person, the very same person, I suspect, who necessitated your visit to this fine vessel, messed me around and set me almost impossible tasks. She has my dogs, if you are not aware, and is threatening to throw them overboard if I fail to comply with her demands."

This was news to him as well, but he wasn't going to back down easily.

"I hardly see how that justifies attacking a member of the crew and taking his sidearm, Mrs Fisher."

I smiled devilishly. "Angelica has members of the crew working for her." Mr Torrance recoiled as if I'd slapped his face. "At this time, I do not know who, but since Angelica created the bogus report of a missing child and played the role of the helpless mother who you were foolish enough to believe I'd killed, you'll have to forgive me if I feel unwilling to trust people."

I locked eyes with Mr Torrance and dared him to argue.

After a three count, I looked down, brushed some imaginary crumbs from the sheets, and started afresh.

"As the ship's detective, I am faced with many different crimes, all of which demand my full attention. In the last week alone, my team have solved a plethora of cases, all of which had to be investigated under the shadow of a psychotic woman hell bent on revenge. I am now on the cusp of catching her and the only thing stopping me is you. However," I added as he recoiled in horror again. "I welcome your oversight."

Alistair, Barbie, in fact everyone in the sickbay gave me an incredulous look.

"My reputation and ability have been called into question amid accusations levied falsely by Angelica Howard-Box. She employed a team of people, reaching out through her contacts and using her own money to place people on board this ship so they could report ill behaviour on my part and a failure to conduct my duties adequately."

"You have proof of this?" he asked, his tone now one of disbelief but the kind that suspected he was finally hearing the truth.

"I am coming to it," I replied to stop the conversation from vanishing on a tangent. "Angelica's crimes are minimal, though it will be possible to prove she was behind a physical attack on my butler, Special Rating Clarke. In addition, she broke into my suite to take my dogs and injured Lieutenant Kashmir in the process. Furthermore, she has illegally hacked into several of the ship's systems including the CCTV."

Alistair frowned, "Really?"

I gave him a sorry nod. "I think so, yes. It is the only thing I can come up with to explain how she constantly knows where I am and what I am doing. She had a man following me ..."

Barbie motioned that she wanted to say something on that subject, but I needed to finish my point about Angelica and my pursuit of her first.

"We'll circle back to him in a moment, sweetie," I assured her. "Because Angelica's crimes were aimed at me, I believed she was a lesser priority than solving murders, thefts, and other crimes on board. In retrospect, I believe I was correct, but should, nevertheless, have dealt with her sooner. I hope you can believe that my team and I tried to find her, but due to the certainty that she has at least one accomplice among the crew, and what I suspect to be a skilful hacker in her employment, she has been able to disguise that she was even on the ship."

"That's preposterous," argued Mr Torrance. "No one can do that."

Barbie turned her wheelchair around to face him, forcing Pippin and Schneider to scoot out of her way.

"I could do that with my laptop in about five minutes. Once a person hacks into the central registry, it's a simple matter of changing a few lines of information. You could even swap out a photo." She swung around to look at me again. "That's what I wanted to tell you about the person you asked us to find. He's not in the system either. I narrowed it down to a few possibles, but Martin and the team checked each of them and they all had solid alibis. Oh, I also need to tell you about Professor Noriega," she revealed.

I wanted to press on and stick with the issue of Angelica, but her comment had intrigued me too greatly for it to be ignored.

"What about him?"

"He's dead," she remarked, but I could tell she wasn't about to leave it at that.

Mr Torrance piped up, "Who is Professor Noriega? Please tell me that is not the name of a passenger."

I shot him a disparaging look to shut him up and raised my eyebrows at Barbie, encouraging her to continue.

"He'd died a week before he got on the ship. The man who attacked us was not the real professor." This was news. "Not only that, his research assistant died the previous day in a separate incident. We can talk more later, but I thought you would like to know.”

I absorbed the information, but didn't let it slow me down.

Alistair had taken himself to one side and was talking in hushed but urgent tones to someone via the ship's phone at the sickbay's reception desk. My guess about the ship's CCTV system demanded he have people look into it immediately.

I thanked Barbie and licked my lips, taking my time to refocus my gaze on the small man from Purple Star headquarters. Composed, I delivered my plan.

“This is what is going to happen now.”

Fighting Back

"Patricia?" Angelica said my name with surprise in her voice.

"Yes. If you are wondering where I have been, I passed out when the tattooing started and ended up cuffed to a bed in sickbay."

"Yes, Patricia, I know what happened. How is it that you are not in the brig, Patricia? Have you broken the rules and taken help from those interfering friends of yours? That would be cheating, Patricia."

"I didn't get help, okay?" Angelica had no idea, but she had just told me her spy web didn't know my friends had all been in the sickbay with me. She was only guessing. Had she known, she would have been screaming insults at me. "I escaped."

"Oh, nonsense, Patricia. How could someone like you escape? First you tell everyone you're a super sleuth, now you think you're a spy."

"Did you really think the ship's detective wouldn't have her own key? I slipped past my guards and here I am, on the run again. Do you want me to try the tattoo thing again, or do you have an even worse task for me to perform? You could, of course, you know, just give me back my dogs and call it even." My voice carried the begging tone of a person who knew they were beaten.

"I think not, Patricia."

That was fine by me. I was at the stage where I would almost rather catch her than have her give in. I was back roaming the ship, but if you expect to hear that the ship's security teams were no longer looking for me then you are sadly mistaken.

I'd convinced Mr Torrance of my innocence and could have the order to catch me rescinded, but certain Angelica had one or more crewmembers in her employment, I couldn't risk tipping her off. She had to believe that she was in charge and winning, right up until my team kicked in the door she was hiding behind. So far as the crew was concerned, I'd escaped and was to be detained on sight once more.

I got help getting out of the crew decks, obviously, and found my way back to the sundecks by use of a freight elevator. Schneider and Pippin went with me to make sure the coast was clear, but when I arrived back among the passengers, I was on my own.

It helped when Alistair confirmed his tech people had discovered a ghost signal in the ship's CCTV system. Someone had hacked into it and was piggybacking the feed. It allowed whoever it was to patch into the cameras around the ship. They were wide angled for the most part, and recorded onto a giant hard drive so that, should it ever be necessary to review events in a particular area, the footage could be accessed and examined.

I pointed out how it explained Angelica's desire to have me dress like an idiot in the pink anime kitten outfit and dye my hair – it made me easy to spot. She had someone following me on foot as a just in case, but was doing her best to watch me – like a god – from on high.

Mr Torrance, given zero choice by Alistair anyway, confirmed he was content to observe. Lieutenants Harvey and Nichols were detained, not because I suspected them; they were too dumb and brutish for Angelica to employ, but because they couldn't be trusted to keep their mouths shut. They would blab about what was going on, a secret that we needed to keep from reaching Angelica's ears until it was too late for her to avoid the inevitable.

My role was to keep Angelica's attention focused on what I was doing. Well, that and staying out of the security team's clutches. Martin and the team were running interference for me, reporting Patricia sightings at other parts of the ship while coordinating with me by radio – yes, they'd given me a radio which I was keeping out of sight. I had my own phone too, which was good because I was going to need it.

Apart from keeping the ship's security detachment off my back, the team was getting ready to mount an assault on a cabin on the eighth deck. They just needed to figure out which one it was.

When I showed them the proof of life picture Angelica sent me of my dogs, they all knew instantly which deck she was on. It was one of those small details she wouldn't have known to keep secret. However, as I said earlier, I could only narrow it down to about two hundred cabins. To narrow it down further, we needed to find the young Asian man.

I apologised that I had not been more exact with my description. I had gotten a better look at him since I begged Marsha to deliver the first note.

"Chinese, but probably mixed race," I offered. "If not Chinese then very close geographically. His accent was English though."

The description was relatively unnecessary because I knew where he had been and when – right on my tail for most of the last twenty-four hours. Using the CCTV footage, they found him in minutes, the radio in my bag squawked to let me know.

They also confirmed he did not appear anywhere in the ship's central registry, which I rather liked and wished I'd been there to see what Mr Torrance's face did.

While I was talking to Angelica and keeping her distracted, they were quizzing the cleaning crews and the stewards. Between those two, they would be able to identify which cabin our mystery man was staying in. I just needed to hope they did it fast.

Angelica continued to gloat, but she said, "Don't worry, Patricia," in a semi-soothing tone. "This will all be over soon. I'm afraid though, that I have more tasks for you yet. You spent so long lying to so many people while you pretended to be something you are not. Surely, you know deep inside that you deserve to suffer?"

I knew no such thing, and I wanted to curse at her for her continual need to be cruel. Now was not the time to challenge her, so I opted to be meek instead. Believing my ordeal was close to reaching an end, I did something I suspected I had probably never once done in my life - I apologised to Angelica Howard-Box.

"I'm sorry, Angelica. Truly I am. Please don't hurt my dogs."

"Finally, you accept the truth. I think perhaps I might make this your final task. If you complete this successfully, I will tell you where you can find your dogs. However, getting caught by security doesn't count, Patricia. Do you understand? They will be looking for you doubly hard now that you have escaped once. You are to do everything in your power to avoid them. Do you want to know what your final task is?"

In an appropriately meek and miserable voice, I said, "Yes, please."

"Very good. I much prefer this new version of Patricia. This is more like the one who used to mope about East Malling married to Charlie Fisher. I could have tolerated her."

Truthfully, Angelica had tolerated me, and I had avoided her because she had money, nice clothes, and a nice car and was ready to throw it all in my face for imagined slights from our childhood. She was right about my current act being more like the Patricia she'd known – being married to Charlie for three decades had slowly eroded the fire in my belly until there was little left of the real me. Only catching him in bed with my best friend had proven to be sufficient shock to break the spell and set me free.

Well, I am free. Free to be the woman I was always meant to be, and Angelica was going to get to see just who that was with both barrels.

Not content to destroy my life, Angelica wanted to ensure I faced my future without the support of my friends. On top of avoiding the entire ship's complement of security, I now had to break into the evidence locker and frame my closest friends as part of a drugs distribution ring I was running. It was Angelica's coup de gras and it wouldn't work, but I doubted the point was to convince anyone they were guilty. Her desire was to make it appear as though I was prepared to betray them. She wanted to alienate me and would go to any length to achieve it.

"Remember," she chose to coach me before she ended the call, "I can see you."

She could see me because we couldn't kick her out of the ship's CCTV system. To do so would blind her, but might also make her believe we were moving against her, and I couldn't have that.

Not yet.

The micro bikini continued to attract unwanted attention, but the shame or embarrassment I'd felt about being seen in it had faded. Those emotions were being replaced by righteous indifference as I rose above the trivial elements of my ordeal.

I set off, heading back inside the ship's structure as I pretended to obey Angelica's latest demand, and I felt buoyant. We were going to get her, and she had no idea it was coming.

179

Childish Need

Every time my radio made a noise, my heart skipped a beat. It was tuned to a different channel than the one employed by the security team, increasing the likelihood that we would be able to communicate secretly.

I was listening for it, telling myself to be patient even though the totality of my existence currently hinged on getting the nod that they'd found the right cabin and were about to spoil Angelica's day.

When it finally came, I was in between hiding places. In my effort to stay concealed from roving patrols of ship's security I was moving slowly and trying to stay out of sight. However, if I assumed Angelica was watching me, I also needed to make it look like I was trying to obey her demands.

"Patty," Barbie's muffled voice drifted out of my handbag. "We've found it. One of the stewards is one hundred percent certain he has the right cabin. I checked it against the ship's registry, and it looks like the passenger listed as staying in that cabin is a fake ID. Not only that, he said the man staying there has a middle-aged woman with him and swears he heard dogs barking yesterday when he delivered food."

I felt like punching the air in victory. I didn't, reining in my jubilant emotions for fear Angelica might see them. I felt good though, magnificent even. We were on the brink of victory.

Spotting a ladies' restroom, I dashed inside, yanking out my radio the moment I was out of sight. There were no CCTV cameras inside the toilets. Obviously.

"Barbie," I hissed into the radio, too cautious to speak at normal volume. "How soon is this going to happen?"

I could hear the smile on her face when she said, "Any minute now. The six of them went down to get in position already."

"Six of them?" there were four in my team. With Sam included, it only made five, and though I loved him dearly and would never put limits on what he could do, I wasn't content to give him a firearm; breaching Angelica's cabin would require precisely that.

Barbie satisfied my curiosity. "The captain is with them. I guess he felt he had a personal need to see this concluded."

My heart swelled.

"Okay," I replied. "I'm going to call her now. I want to hear when they bust her." Was it childish need that made me want to listen when

Angelica realised her grand scheme was all over and was ending in failure? Maybe, but I didn't care. There was no coming back from this for her. She would face criminal charges for her assaults on Jermaine and Kashmir ... the back of my skull itched.

I needed to think about that, but it could wait. I thanked Barbie, locked myself inside one of the stalls and used the burner phone to call Angelica.

"Patricia," she acknowledged me without greeting. "Are you calling me to say your task is complete? You have not had enough time yet, surely?"

I tried to keep the excitement from my voice, when I replied. "No, Angelica, that's not why I am calling. I hoped we might discuss what happens next."

"You will be incarcerated, Patricia. You will, of course, claim your actions were under duress, and produce the phone I gave you as evidence. However, the phone and any other indication that there was someone controlling your movements will miraculously vanish while you are locked up and the testimony of your friends, if they testify at all once you have betrayed them, will not be enough to change the course of events. You will finally get what you deserve."

"How much planning did you put into this, Angelica? How much money?" I wanted to hear her voice when Alistair kicked in her door and for that I needed her to be talking.

"Why are you asking?" Her voice was filled with suspicion.

"Because you have beaten me, Angelica," I told her a lie I believed she would like. "I'm still reeling from it. I don't see a way to escape the trap you set for me."

"Are you trying to congratulate me?" she asked, her head swelling with pride.

I choked, "Not exactly. I just want to know how you did it."

"Ha!" she spat. "Like a master criminal in a movie revealing all their dastardly plans? I don't think so, Patricia."

I pressed on, my heart beating fast from the anticipation. Any second now I would hear her gasp or squeal in shock as my friends smashed their way into her cabin.

"What about crew, Angelica? You must have at least one or two working for you. How else could you have pulled this off? How else could you have avoided the search party when I sent them to scour the ship one cabin at a time?"

"It only took one, Patricia," she bragged, and finally she was telling me her secrets. "Just one member of crew, one of your beloved security people. He was good enough to accept a fee far less than I was willing to pay. In truth, I ought to have rejected him for not being mercenary enough."

And now I knew it was a man though the odds had always leaned that way – the crew is more than sixty percent male.

What was taking so long? Was it just me or was time stretching out? Surely, they had to be in position by now. Telling myself they had probably hit a snag with passengers in the passageway outside her cabin and needed to clear them first, I probed a little further.

"How did you find out about Hennessey? How did you know to contact her?"

My radio hissed; that small static noise it always makes when someone had pressed their send button and was about to talk. I had it turned right down, but worried Angelica might hear, I clamped my hand over the phone to drown out what was going to be said.

Barbie's voice said, "Patty?"

In Position

<hr>

Eight decks below me and on the other side of the ship, Lieutenant Commander Martin Baker was getting everyone into position. Deepa and Pippin had been sent to either end of the passageway to keep passengers away. They would politely advise that the crew had to bar access for now.

"It will only be for a few minutes," Deepa assured a couple who were returning to their cabin after several hours in the sun. They wanted to clean up before lunch and they could do that. They just needed to wait until the bust had taken down Angelica.

That they had the right cabin was in no question. They had taken the extra time – despite the pressure they felt to end Patricia's ordeal – to triple check who was staying in each of the possible cabins and to be one hundred percent certain the passenger in 0896 had never been seen by anyone. There was no record of him ever leaving the ship at any of the ports and he had been onboard for almost a month.

In the end, Alistair made the call, making it his responsibility if they were wrong.

Silence ruled the passageway as Martin held up a fist and extended three fingers. Standing to the left of the handle, Ensign Sam Chalk held a universal key card. His task was to swipe it against the lock. Directly in front of the door, lined up and touching the shoulder of the man in front, were Lieutenant Schneider, Lieutenant Commander Baker, and Captain Huntley.

Baker's finger folded inward, three, two, one. The lock clicked open, and the three men barged through the door.

Down and then Up

My head was spinning. "What do you mean she's not there?" I hissed into the radio. Angelica's voice was coming over my phone, too muffled to make out with my hand clamped over it, but there all the same and becoming impatient.

Barbie sounded awful when she apologised again. "I'm sorry, Patty. It's the right cabin. The guys are saying there's evidence that both she and the dogs were there. They found some of your clothing and jewellery, and they found the young Asian man's passport. His real name is Jordan Jones, but Angelica either went for a walk and is about to return or she knew we were coming and left.

I had to respond to Angelica. If she was still tapped into the CCTV feed, then she knew the cabin had just been raided.

However, Barbie alleviated some of my worries when she told me, "The guys said the cabin is set up like an airport control tower. There are computers and monitors everywhere and whoever that Jordan guy is, he built himself a server to control it all. Like literally built it in the cabin. Wherever Angelica is now, I don't think she has access to the ship's CCTV any longer."

I slumped against the wall of the stall, feeling tension I was barely admitting to myself, seeping from my body. Only for a moment though. Angelica had left the cabin of her own accord and we could station people inside in case she returned. However, I was willing to bet she had a backup cabin somewhere.

"I'll call you back in a minute," I hissed, ending the call, and switching the radio off. "Angelica, I have to go. I think I just heard someone call for security. I guess I was spotted. I'm on deck eighteen and need to get to the crew decks."

"I don't care, Patricia. I don't need to hear your problems. Just get the job done or die trying." She ended the call without another word but had told me plenty - I lied about my location, and she didn't say a word.

She really didn't have access to the CCTV anymore. It was a small thing, but without Jordan following me, it only left the slim possibility that her turncoat security officer might be following.

Now that I was free to talk, I turned the radio on again.

"Barbie?" I called to get her attention.

Alistair answered. "Patricia. Where are you? Are you okay?"

"I'm fine. I'm just frustrated. We came close, but I don't think she will be far away. She admitted to having help …" I told Alistair, and the rest of my friends who I knew would be listening, about our most recent conversation. A male member of crew, almost certainly a member of the ship's security detachment, was working for Angelica. He would have been involved in getting her onto the ship, in helping her avoid detection when we searched the entire ship trying to find her, and in keeping tabs on me now.

I believed that since we'd found both Hennessey and Jordan were staying in cabins on deck eight, Angelica wouldn't be all that far away, and with a spark of vision, I believed I knew just how to find her.

Excited, now that I could see a solution to my problem, I said, "Stay there. I'm on my way to you."

Running as I left the ladies' restroom and holding my boobs to keep them from jiggling clean out of my stupid bikini, I had to force myself to slow down. She had the dogs with her, and they were on deck eight. The team had eliminated a bunch of cabins from the two hundred or so I had narrowed it down to, and what was left presented a manageable search vector.

Not that I would have to search. The dogs would react to the sound of my voice, and they would certainly react to the smell of food. I wasn't to employ either of those tactics though. If there was one thing that got them off the couch and running every single time, it was the sound of their treat jar moving.

It didn't seem to matter how asleep they were, they could hear it and would come running, their excitement at the possibility of a gravy bone accentuated by whining and, if no treat were forthcoming, insistent barking.

All I had to do was walk around on deck eight and rattle their treat jar, Anna and Georgie would do the rest.

Barbie radioed to confirm she had the jar of gravy bones and was wheeling herself at speed for the nearest elevator.

Oh, yeah, we were going to get Angelica despite the most recent set back, and I hadn't even had to employ my final nuclear, blow-Angelica-out-of-the-water tactic. Not that I had it in my arsenal yet – I was still waiting for the call.

From feeling beaten and depressed to riding a wave of jubilant joy once again, I soon came crashing down to earth once more when I turned the next corner and saw what was waiting for me.

Cursed Technology

"Just one more day," Angelica told the doggies. "Twenty-four hours from now we will be docking in Rio de Janeiro. I haven't been there in years. It will be so nice to spend some time relaxing once this is over."

Anna and Georgie, still confused about where they were, yet content because nothing bad was happening to them, wagged their tails as the woman chattered to them. Like most dogs, they lived in the present and spent little time reflecting on the past. They were curious about where their usual human had gotten to, but this new person kept giving them chicken.

Angelica had changed her stance on the dogs and their future. They were cute and friendly, and she liked having someone to talk to who didn't interrupt or question what she was saying. If she could, she was going to take them with her tomorrow when she left the ship.

Doing so came with a degree of risk – however, the security officer she employed showed complete confidence when quizzed about the final element of his work. He was going to take her off through the royal suites' exit, employing a technique to distract the guards who would be manning it.

Escaping her confines was long overdue so far as Angelica was concerned, not least because her arrangements were beginning to unravel. Patricia's claim about Jordan appeared to be true and Angelica found that deeply aggravating.

He hadn't answered his phone when she called or responded to any of her messages. His decision to abscond hadn't come as that much of a shock – he'd been acting squirrely for days. It was why she'd taken his passport ... with an angry groan, she realised she hadn't collected it from its hiding place when she left Jordan's cabin.

Whether she needed to move cabins or not was something Angelica was still debating, but unwilling to trust that Jordan wouldn't get caught now that Patricia knew who he was, Angelica opted for caution.

Regardless, Angelica believed Jordan had gone and wasn't coming back. It didn't matter; he'd served his purpose. Patricia was all but beaten and enough damage had been done between the resignation letter, the crimes Patricia had been forced to commit and the ...

Angelica paused. What had happened to the video Patricia recorded? Originally, Angelica had expected to force Patricia to rerecord and rerecord it until she got it right, but surprisingly her first attempt had been a doozie. Okay, Patricia didn't look anywhere near deranged enough and Angelica had planned to have her do it again wearing her new hair and outfit. However, when Angelica saw what Patricia looked like after the makeover, she changed her mind.

Patricia Fisher looked so different with pink hair and the ridiculous costume that Angelica questioned whether internet conspiracy theorists might question if it was really her. She'd meant to have Jordan post the original confession video, but by then he was out tailing Patricia and when he returned much later that night, it had slipped Angelica's mind.

Angelica picked up her laptop. Could she do it? Technology had never been her friend, but she knew she had the original confession video – Jordan had played it for her, and she knew how to use her computer for things like email and such.

Come to think of it, Angelica acknowledged, the time had come to transfer some money around. Hiding on board the vast cruise ship, she'd known she couldn't use her credit cards to pay for things so had arrived with an abundance of cash. Paying off Jordan was easy enough using internet banking, but it was time now to shift funds into her current account ready for some time ashore.

She would give herself a week before flying home. That was enough time to relax and rejuvenate after so long away from the sun.

She looked first at the video Patricia recorded, watching it through once more just because it gratified her to do so. Thereafter though, she found she was stuck. Upload it to YouTube? Was that what Jordan said? Angelica had heard of the platform, but that was all. An internet search found what she wanted after a couple of attempts to spell the silly name correctly.

What now though?

Cursing at the screen for stubbornly refusing to highlight what she needed to press, Angelica gave up and opened her banking app. At least she knew how to work that one.

However, a frown formed when she accessed her account. There was something wrong. It was showing zero funds. Blinking in her confusion, Angelica checked the details, coming out of her account and going back in only to find the same line of zeroes showing where yesterday there had been a significant pot of savings.

It took a few more seconds before the penny dropped, the dogs both jumping to their paws when the lady in the cabin screamed, "Jordan!"

Run for Your Life

My feet dug into the short pile carpet that lines the public passenger areas of the ship, but it was too late to avoid being seen. Spider Williams and his remaining bodyguard, Ralph, had been waiting for the elevator. They both turned their heads when I rounded the corner at speed, their eyes drawn by the noise of sudden movement. They performed double takes, starting to look away again when their brains caught up with the message their eyeballs supplied.

"You," growled Spider.

That they were going to give chase did not need to be explained and it was fortunate that I was already more or less running because they started toward me instantly.

"I know who you are, Patricia Fisher!" he shouted at my back. "You were trying to get me to confess to a murder I didn't commit! Another scalp for your wall, was I?"

So he'd figured out who I was. That didn't come as much of a shock. That he was chasing me didn't either, but what was he planning to do if he caught me? Let's just say I wasn't going to ask him and wouldn't have trusted his answer if he gave one.

Running, quite possibly, for my life, I couldn't pump my arms for extra speed without letting go of my chest. I didn't want to do that, but could already hear that the younger and fitter of the two men in pursuit was gaining on me.

Ralph would catch me if I didn't go faster, so with a growl of annoyance, I uncupped my boobs and let them do what gravity and inertia did best. The top half of the micro bikini fought to stay in place for roughly half a nanosecond before finding a new position where it felt more comfortable – underneath my boobs.

Now able to put in extra effort, not that it was comfortable running without support for my chest, I went faster, but Ralph was still gaining.

In a passageway heading aft on the starboard side of the ship, I expected to run into passengers, and I did.

Two boys, the same ones I stole the scooter from last night, I realised, stepped out of their cabin with their parents. The boys got an eyeful as did the dad, who like his sons took a moment to appreciate the view.

I cursed and tutted, but I didn't slow down. The boys were shouting – they recognised who I was, and the younger kid wanted his scooter back.

That made dad shout too, his angry words aimed at my back. I wanted to shout an apology and promise to make it up to them as had always been my intention, but I had no breath to spare on words. They were going to call security and the description of a mad, pink-haired, topless woman would bring armed officers to my location faster than a fire.

Of course, with things as bad as they were, in true Patricia Fisher style, they then got worse.

A shadow darkened the glass panel of the double doors I was heading for. I knew they led to another set of passageways and more passenger accommodation, but something about the height and girth of the shadows bothered me. I found out why a heartbeat later when Greg pushed the left hand door open. Laney came through the right hand door and they both saw me at the same moment.

Squealing in fright, I couldn't figure out what to do. Greg was limping, his groin bulging with what I had to guess were bandages.

"You circumcised me!" he bellowed, his rage off the scale.

Laney, her face equally contorted with blind anger, shouted, "She got our stash confiscated, Greg! That's a darned sight more crucial than your tiny todger. Ship's security is looking for us, we've no way off this stinking vessel without getting caught, Roger is already in custody, and she ruined our entire operation. Focus on what's important!"

Screeching to a stop, I turned hard right. Ralph was five yards away and maybe three seconds from grabbing me. Laney, running to get to me as well, though Greg was limping and couldn't keep up, would arrive half a second after Ralph.

I had one shot at getting away.

I hadn't seen it until the very last second, but to my right, hidden between the line of cabin doors was a cross passage. I ran down it, my pursuers following a moment later. It took me toward the centre axis of the ship and away from the passenger cabins. Located amidships were the services such as water and electricity coming up from the warehouse-sized storerooms in the belly of the ship.

Leaving the last of the passenger cabins behind, I exited the cross passage and jinked to my left. Throwing in some turns Ralph wasn't expecting prevented him from closing the distance, but now I had deliberately led them away from the passengers, I needed to find a way to lose them for good.

The idea in my head was too loose to warrant the term 'plan' but it was all I had. My phone rang, the noise coming from deep inside my handbag which clattered and bashed against my left hip as I ran. I could use it to beg help from whoever was calling, but it got ignored because I'd just seen my salvation.

Ripping the universal key card from my handbag, I swiped at the door I had spotted and fell through it, kicking it shut with both feet a fraction of a second before something heavy hit the outside.

I'd landed in a cleaners' storeroom. It was where they parked their cleaning carts overnight before reloading them in the morning with fresh linen, towels, and toiletries. I was safe for now, but when Greg caught up, would the door hold?

Ralph swore inventively, the voice of Laney joining him just a moment later.

My phone rang off and the caller hung up rather than leave a message. I expected to see Barbie's name displayed as a missed call, but it wasn't her and it wasn't my phone. It was the burner phone and though the caller was displayed only as a number, I was willing to bet it had been exactly who I wanted to talk to. If I was right, then Felicity had come through for me and the caller was the one person who could end Angelica's reign of terror.

I had missed the call.

Getting to my feet, I snatched a cleaner's tabard left hanging on the handle of a cart. It wasn't clean, but it covered my top half better than the stupid bikini had and that was good enough. Hastily arranging the hybrid apron/jacket so it hid as much flesh as possible, I was about to return the missed call when my phone started ringing again.

I thumbed the green button and pressed it to my ear, trying to drown out the shouting and thumping coming from the other side of the door.

I said, "This is Patricia Fisher. Hello?" hoping I wasn't about to be deeply disappointed.

A man's voice asked a simple question. "Mrs Fisher, is it true?"

What Angelica did not see Coming

I had to explain what had been happening, but I didn't have to go to any great lengths to convince the person I was talking to. In fact, it seemed my story came as little surprise.

Outside the door, as I tried to conduct my conversation, Greg had arrived, and a discussion had ensued. They could hear me talking, but believed I was trapped and would have to come out eventually.

Greg tried the door, slamming into it with enough force to make the frame rattle. One thing about the ship is that the structure is largely steel for rigidity. Interior walls in the cabins were wood and plaster, much like one might find in a house, but where I was, in a storage area away from the usual places passengers would go, it was steel all the way.

Greg would get through eventually, but I had bought myself some time. How much time, I couldn't know, but I hoped it would be enough to do what was necessary.

Putting the burner phone to one side with the call still connected, I placed a second call on my own phone, this time to the number I had for Angelica. There had existed a mild concern she wouldn't answer when she saw the new number and to overcome that I sent her a text first so she would know it was me.

"Patricia," she snapped out my name. "Are you calling from your own phone? How are you now in possession of it? Have you been getting help from your friends? You are in forfeit!"

"Slow down, Angelica," I implored. "Yes, I have my own phone. I needed it, you see. We are coming to the close of things, wouldn't you s ay?"

Typically, my arch nemesis sneered, "That depends on you, Patricia. I will release your dogs when you complete your final task. Don't tell me you have done so already because I won't believe you. I will know when it is done."

"Because you bribed a member of the ship's security to spy for you and help you arrange your hidden passage aboard this vessel?"

"Precisely."

I sighed and readied myself for what I was about to do. I didn't really want to ... it's not like she deserved the chance I was going to give her, but it wasn't in my nature to play the hangman. That was what

Angelica would do, lofting herself to a haughty position where she believed her world view was the only one that mattered.

No, if Angelica's neck was going into the proverbial noose, she was going to be the one to put it there.

"Are you sure you want to do this Angelica? Are you certain you would not rather come clean about what you have been doing and set my dogs free now? The charges against you will be less severe if you give yourself up."

She laughed, her voice loud in the enclosed space as it played over the speaker on my phone. I had set it like that so the person on the other call could hear her words.

"What do I have to fear, Patricia? Soon you will be incarcerated, and whether you complete this final task and earn back your dogs, it will be years before you see them again. Now if you'll excuse me, I need to send my tame security guard to kill the hacker I brought on board. It seems he has chosen to misbehave."

"Mother."

The single word, spoken by Bobbie Howard-Box, premiership football star, poster child for British sports in general, and Angelica's only son, stopped Angelica dead in her tracks like dropping a mountain in front of a freight train.

She said nothing, the seconds stretching out until she questioned what she had heard.

"Bobbie?"

"Yes, Mother," he sighed, his voice heavy with the shame and regret he felt. "Mother what are you doing?"

Her tone and attitude changed in an instant. "Bobbie, how lovely to hear your voice ..."

"Stop it," he growled.

"Did I forget to mention I was taking a trip. After that debacle of a wedding, I really needed to get away. Get some sun on my skin ..."

"Stop!" he raised his voice.

"I was just having a little chat with Patricia Fisher. Joking around about some things. Did you know she works on a cruise ship now?"

"MOTHER!" Bobbie's angry bellow silenced her. "I knew you were a bully and a vengeful cow with a belly full of spite, but I had no idea you could stoop to committing crime to get what you wanted!"

"Darling," she cooed. "You don't know what you are saying ..."

He cut her off again, each of his shouts like a slap to Angelica's face. Angelica was everything Bobbie had just said and much, much more. The hatred inside her had no outlet – there was no joy in her life to help it to dissipate, and it boiled and squirmed inside her desperate to be unleashed.

If it hadn't been aimed at me, it would have been someone else.

It pained me to have involved Bobbie; he was a sweet young man with a promising future, but I knew the position he held in his mother's heart. She wouldn't be able to carry on with her evil plans now that he knew.

Drifting away as she continued to try to lie to him and he called her out every time, I took the radio from my bag.

Trapped in a storeroom on deck sixteen, I back away from the door. There was nothing more I could do about Angelica other than to hope my friends would find her.

Pressing the send button, I fixed my voice to sound hopeful and bright, before saying, "Hey, everyone, it's Patricia."

The only people listening on this channel were supposed be my friends, and that proved to be most likely the case when Alistair was the first to answer.

"Darling, where are you? Barbie is here already."

"Um, kind of trapped. I'm still on deck sixteen."

Barbie cut in, "Trapped? Trapped how?"

Jermaine was next. "Madam, please tell me where you are, and I will come directly to you."

I gave them my location, but made it quite clear they could not hope to get to me before it was too late to matter.

"I'm in the midships cleaners' storeroom on deck sixteen, but please don't worry, I have a plan." It wasn't necessarily a lie. "Please focus on finding Angelica and get my dogs back."

Alistair argued and he wasn't the only one, but I stopped them all with a simple instruction.

"They are going to break through the door any moment now and I want to be able to concentrate on them. I can't talk to you and deal with them. I'm going to try to talk my way out of this."

I flicked a button on the radio. Alistair was saying something, but I cut him off mid word.

In a brief moment of silence, I could hear the faint sound of heated conversation coming from the two phones. I'd placed them side by side on top of a cleaning cart. Mother and son were disagreeing still, but I could hear that Angelica was losing ground.

Bobbie knew what she'd been doing, and I thought I heard him threaten her – something to do with never seeing her grandchild. Did that mean his girlfriend was pregnant?

Their discussion was, however, background noise. Mostly I was hearing the argument raging outside. Spider and Ralph might want the same thing as Greg and Laney, but their partnership was a marriage of convenience.

They were failing to agree on tactics.

"Put your back into it," Laney spoke as if her partner wasn't trying hard enough in his attempts to break through the door.

There was pause in the thumping - Greg was taking a break. "I'm injured," he pointed out. "She shot me."

"She shot you?" questioned Spider Williams. "You don't look shot."

I backed away from the door, looking around and wondering how long I had. I needed more time than they were going to give me, that was almost certainly true.

Greg sounded defensive and a little embarrassed when he admitted, "She shot me in the trousers."

"Oh, please," begged Laney, the only woman in the foursome. "The bullet only grazed the skin."

Greg wasn't content to let her belittle his injury claim.

"She virtually circumcised me with a bullet, Laney." I heard Spider and his bodyguard wince loudly.

When Laney spoke again, it was a verbal rolling of her eyes. "Then she's an amazing shot, Greg. How she managed to hit that tiny thing without blowing it clean off, I'll never know. Steroid abuse did you no favours."

Greg growled with impotent rage, unsurprisingly unhappy to have his manhood discussed in public.

"That's the spirit!" Laney encouraged. "Now get that door open!"

Trapped? Part Two

I believe this is where I originally started to explain events. That seems like a long time ago now.

Spider, Ralph, Greg, and Laney burst through the door and glared at me with murderous eyes. Greg threw a steel pry bar to one side. Where he'd found it was an interesting question, but not one I was about to ask. It clanged and skidded to a stop a few yards away.

My back was against the wall, and they were coming for me. Greg and Laney were out for revenge; it was too late for them to do anything about the fact that I'd unwittingly uncovered the casino chip scam they'd been running. They were going to get caught and they knew it. Hurting me was just for a sense of revenge.

Spider wanted to hurt me too, but only to extract information. Accused of murder, but released when the primary witness up and vanished, Spider believed I'd been trying to coax a confession from him.

To be fair, that was exactly what I had been doing on one of Angelica's stupid tasks, all of which were designed entirely to result in my death, maiming, or imprisonment. Spider Williams needed to be sure there was no one else coming after him, but whether he managed to force information from me or not, he couldn't then allow me to live.

The four were spread out in a line, advancing slowly but confidently.

"Who goes first?" asked Ralph.

"I do," stated Spider, like it should have been obvious.

Greg's brow furrowed and he lifted an arm to bar Spider's path.

"Why do you get to go first? She didn't shoot you. I should get to hurt her first. You can have what's left. I'm the one who got injured."

Laney roared, "Enough. Goodness, it's like working with children. She's the one we want. Let Spider hurt her until she tells him what he wants to know. When he's done, you can toss her overboard. Deal?"

The three men, calmly discussing my murder like they were figuring out what to have for lunch, exchanged looks and shrugs but none of them argued.

It appeared they had reached a decision.

Just as they were about to start toward me, I held up my right hand, palm out.

"Wait!"

All four obeyed and looked surprised at themselves for doing so. I grabbed the chance this created and filled the world with words.

"I'll happily tell you everything you want to know," I blurted, sounding like I was terrified, which wasn't any kind of acting stretch. "You have me cornered in the deck sixteen cleaners' storeroom against the portside bulkhead. The four of you are fanned out roughly a yard apart across the centre of the room. You have me trapped. But there's a couple of things you ought to know before you do what you plan to do."

"Oh, yeah?" growled Greg. "What?"

"Well, first off, I want you to know that I have been an unwitting and reluctant pawn in someone else's game. The things that happened to you were not my fault."

Laney scoffed, "That's the same nonsense you wrote in that note you left in our cabin. I didn't believe it then either. And it hardly makes any difference who was behind it. You're the super sleuth, you're the one who is going to pay."

"Yeah," echoed Greg.

"Okay," I licked my lips nervously. "Well, have you noticed how this door here," I pointed to the one just behind me, "looks a lot like the one you came through." I nodded my head across the room.

All four slowly rotated their torsos to look back at the mangled door.

Spider shrugged. "What about it?"

I had essentially just told them exactly what was going to happen.

"I said there were a couple of things you needed to know." Their attention swung back to me. "In truth, it is three things. Firstly, I've had my finger on the send button of this radio the whole time. Secondly, I've been stalling, and thirdly, this storeroom sits amidships and can be accessed from both sides.

With a flourish, I darted to the door, snatched the handle, and swung it open for the guards outside to rush in.

Nothing happened.

Laney was looking at Greg, Greg was staring at me, and Spider was scratching his head and questioning whether I was safe to be let out in public.

I shot them a nervous grin. "Sorry. I thought there was going to be someone there."

"Kill her now?" Greg asked Spider, the two of them finally agreeing when he nodded his head.

"Yes, I think that would be appropriate," the ageing rocker replied nonchalantly.

The giant cage fighter took one pace toward me, but paused before his back foot lifted off the deck again. He could hear something, and he wasn't the only one.

My would-be killers looked worried for the first time. They were questioning what they could hear, but I wasn't. I knew exactly what it was.

The sound of running feet coming through the open port and starboard doors grew in volume over the next five seconds until dozens of white uniformed security officers burst into the storeroom with their sidearms drawn. They screamed to be obeyed, subduing Spider, Ralph, and Laney in an instant.

Greg roared like a bear and looked around for someone to fight. I thought for a moment that he was going to get himself shot, but mercifully he recognised the inevitability of his situation and surrendered before that became necessary.

I breathed a sigh of relief and moved to rest against a cool steel bulkhead. Only for a second though. That was how long it took me to remember Angelica and my dogs.

The security officers, many of whom had probably spent hours searching for me with orders to apprehend on sight, were led by Commander Pace. I went straight to him.

"Mrs Fisher, the captain relayed everything you said directly to me and had us switch radio channels. That was a clever strategy, telling us where they were in the room. Thank you."

I dipped my head to acknowledge his compliment, but was heading for where I'd left the phones.

"Thank you, Commander Pace. I may yet need your assistance. I need to check on the captain." Neither phone was active; the calls having ended. This was good, but didn't give me the answer I wanted.

I was just about to turn up the volume on my radio to call Alistair when his voice came over Commander Pace's radio instead.

"Commander Pace, this is the captain. Do you have Mrs Fisher? Report."

I gestured for the radio and answered his question myself. "I'm here, Alistair. I'm fine. Do you have my dogs? Did you find Angelica?"

I held my breath, waiting for him to tell me the day was saved, or the worst had happened. Would she? Was Angelica capable of hurting my dogs? What lengths might she go to when she realised it was all over? I had ambushed her with her own son, gambling he would force her to see reason when no one else could.

It was probably only a second between me asking and Alistair providing an answer, yet at the time it seemed to take forever.

"Yes, Patricia. We have your dogs. Anna and Georgie are unharmed."

My knees went on strike, folding out from beneath me as relief tried to rob me of my consciousness. I dropped the radio, which Commander Pace caught, dropped, juggled, and caught again. I would have rather he caught me, but instead I sank to a sitting position on the deck where I stayed for a while.

Commander Pace crouched, coming down to my head height.

"Can I get you a cup of sweet tea, Mrs Fisher?" he crooked a finger at one of his subordinates, calling him across to then send him to fetch me a beverage.

Before the man could set off, I caught the leg of his trousers.

"Gin and tonic," I begged. "I don't need tea. I need gin and tonic."

Catching Up

<hr>

You might think that I wanted to confront Angelica, but nothing could be further from the truth. Alistair assured me she was on her way to the brig and that was good enough for me.

Good enough for now, anyway.

My entire security detachment was taking her. Martin, Schneider, Pippin, Deepa, and Sam; the five of them absolute overkill, but all wanting to see the job done properly. We were all very conscious that we were yet to identify who it was she had on her payroll.

Angelica went to the brig, and I went to my suite, escorted on the captain's instructions by Commander Pace and a detachment of six security officers. Alistair was taking no chances today.

I knew there was work to do still and it was only late afternoon, but carrying a cold glass that had once contained a healthy measure of gin and tonic, and looking like a refugee from a bad night out, I arrived back at my cabin certain I was going to do nothing and go nowhere until I had eaten, imbibed at least another delicious gin and tonic, cleaned myself thoroughly, and found some sensible clothes to wear.

It was the last two that I tackled first because I knew people were heading for my suite. My hair was still wet, and very pink despite a good attempt at washing it all out in one go, when Jermaine and Barbie arrived.

They had Anna and Georgie with them, Anna riding on Barbie's lap only to leap from it the moment she saw me, and Georgie squirming in Jermaine's arms so she could join her mother.

I fell to my knees, letting both dogs climb me. I cried and my face went all blotchy and my nose filled with mucus which then dripped, but I didn't care one jot because I had my dogs back.

Barbie, hopping so she wouldn't disobey her boyfriend/doctor's advice, kept off her bad ankle, but joined me on the carpet where the pair of us shed tears together.

Jermaine was more stoical, maintaining his stiff upper lip though I swear I spotted him dabbing at his eyes with a handkerchief when he thought I wasn't looking.

He made drinks, not just for me, but for Commander Pace and his team who stuck to non-alcoholic beverages as they were on duty.

Technically, I was probably on duty too, but good luck to anyone who wanted to pry the gin and tonic out of my hand.

Alistair was en route, delayed by a detour to collect Mr Torrance. I knew the man from Purple Star HQ was coming – Alistair had already asked me about it. I could have refused to see him until the morning when sleep would have made me feel more human, but I guess I wanted to get all my unpleasant tasks out of the way as swiftly as possible.

Commander Pace left when the captain arrived, the two men exchanging salutes just inside the lobby. Pace took his men with him, leaving five of us in my suite. I whispered to Barbie, revealing a few things she didn't know – to be fair, no one knew – and requested she employ that big brain of hers.

I was prevented from saying anything much else when Alistair pulled me into an embrace. We hugged for several seconds, neither saying anything. We would talk later when we were alone.

"I have something for you," announced the captain of the Aurelia, stepping back and reaching into a pocket.

I watched, curious to see what he was about to produce.

"My necklace!" I exclaimed, gobsmacked to have it back in my possession. Alistair reached up to place it around my neck and I turned so he could see to fasten it.

"We found some of your clothes too," he let me know. How much of it you want back, you can decide later, darling."

That Angelica had taken some of my clothes was unexpected news. When she broke into my suite, she trashed my wardrobe, destroying so much of it that I assumed everything was gone. However, did I really want any of it back? Angelica had touched it and I would be reminded every time I saw it.

It was a problem for tomorrow and I was given no time to consider it further because Mr Torrance, whose first name I learned was Ian, wanted to get on with things.

"All in good time, Ian," I replied. "Cruises are supposed to be a time when we allow the pace of events to slow."

Barbie snorted her drink back into her glass at my comment, almost choking as she tried to wipe drops of gin and tonic from her nose.

"Patty when do we ever get a chance to slow the pace?"

I shrugged. "Just because it never seems to happen, doesn't mean it shouldn't. Anyway," I replied, "I need to eat. Have you eaten dinner, Ian?"

He hadn't expected the question, but it came as no surprise that he had skipped lunch in all the excitement. We all had, and it was almost four o'clock.

Apologising for my behaviour – I refused to get off the couch where I was contently pinned beneath two sleeping dachshunds, and for my insistence that we wait until everyone was here before we discussed Angelica and the events of the last twenty-four hours, I asked Jermaine to make enough food for the whole team.

They arrived in drips and drabs, Sam and his gran, Gloria, beating the others to it. Next came my four security officers, and shortly after them, Hideki, who was technically still on shift as the ship's on-call doctor, but able to slip away.

"Isn't that everyone, darling?" questioned Alistair right before someone knocked on the door.

With a grin, I said, "There's one more. I'll explain why shortly."

The additional person was Molly. Otherwise known as Ensign Lawrie. She didn't know why she had been invited either and I was fine with that – I quite like being secretive and mysterious.

Jermaine had enlisted help from the kitchens, delegating the task of producing a banquet rather than slaving to produce it himself. I had requested he do so several times in the past, but this was the first time he'd seen fit to comply. As we all fell hungrily upon the food, I encouraged Alistair to regale the audience with Angelica's final moments of freedom.

Alistair, together with Martin and his team were on deck eight when Barbie arrived with the jar of gravy bones from my cabin. Cleverly, the team all used their phones to record her rattling the tin before setting off in different directions. With seven of them working on it simultaneously, it was no surprise that they found my dogs in under two minutes.

However, Alistair deferred to Deepa at that point for she was the one who found Angelica and it wasn't the dogs that gave her location away.

Deepa heard Angelica crying.

I was right about hearing Bobbie say there was a grandchild on the way. Teagan was pregnant, the couple over the moon and freshly engaged to be married, a situation that would have occurred months or even years ago had Angelica not intervened because she thought she knew best.

When the dogs whined at the sound of their treat jar rattling, Deepa swiped the door lock with her universal key card while barking into her radio and training her sidearm on Angelica's centre of mass.

I found Deepa, a former Pakistani infantry soldier and sniper, a little scary sometimes, but in a good way, I suppose. It was comforting to know she was by my side when things got dangerous.

I closed my eyes and tried to put myself in a mental safe space when Deepa and the rest of Martin's team talked about Angelica. The things she had forced me to do, the things she said about me ... they were going to stay with me as emotional scars for the rest of my life.

Angelica was silent on her way to the brig and said not one word during processing. She was yet to be interviewed; my request that everyone come to my suite taking precedence over formalities which could be conducted later. Letting her stew was a good tactic.

With Angelica's story covered adequately, attention turned to me. My friends all wanted to hear what they had missed. For most of the last day I had been out of contact and out of sight. When I reappeared, I had pink hair and was dressed in the world's smallest bikini. I still needed to figure out who I'd stolen that from, but that was for later too.

They'd heard the reports of me being seen in the pink anime kitten outfit racing through the ship on a child's stolen scooter – another wrong I needed to right - and wanted to know what the heckity heck had occurred.

I started with my letter of resignation.

Alistair spat out his tea.

It made me laugh, amusement a welcome emotion.

"It was Angelica's first task," I explained, following that up with her reference to Hercules. "She insisted I had to resign from my job, sending an email to Purple Star's HR department and my second task was to send her a video of me confessing to being a total fraud."

"But you're not a fraud, madam," argued Jermaine.

Barbie flapped an arm in his direction to stop him talking.

"Don't worry, babes, the resignation was made under duress. The captain can rescind it, right, Sir?"

"No need," I remarked, downing the last of my gin and tonic. With all eyes on me, I explained, "I changed one letter in the email address. It went out, but it was never going to reach its destination. That will work, right?" I questioned, suddenly less than certain I was as clever as I thought.

Barbie smiled and nodded her head. "Yes, Patty, that will work just fine. What about the video though?" Her fingers were flying over her phone's screen, typing something in as she tried to find it.

She was not alone, and it was Sam who commented first.

"I can't find anything?" he remarked, his eyebrows knitted together.

Alistair agreed, "There's nothing new here at all, Patricia."

I allowed myself to breathe a sigh of relief; it seemed I had dodged two bullets so far.

Our meal was done, and though the three gin and tonics I'd drunk so far were calling insistently for more to join the party going on in my bloodstream, I could not allow myself any more. Like I said earlier, the day wasn't done yet. There was more work to do, and it really wouldn't do to make it wait.

Turning to Barbie, I asked, "How did you get on with the thing?"

Demands

"What are we doing now?" Ian Torrance wanted to know. Out of everyone in my suite, he was very much the outsider. That wasn't going to change, but I included him in our operation because I needed him to understand what he was seeing before he took a report back to Purple Star.

Cryptically, I said, "All will be revealed very soon, Ian," and deferred to Barbie.

My blonde friend had indeed been successful with the 'thing' and had a recording to play to the room. It needed an introduction first.

Addressing the room, though the show and tell was largely for Ian's benefit, Barbie said, "Patricia asked me to retrieve something from the cloud earlier. It's a recording Patty took with her phone, but before I play it, I need to ask if you are all familiar with the Spider Williams' case?"

Molly raised a hand. "I'm not," she admitted, her cheeks tinged with red when she realised hers was the only hand raised. "Who is that?"

She got a very quick rundown on the pertinent points and Barbie played the recording while I explained about Angelica's fourth task.

"What you do know is that Angelica tasked me with obtaining the confession US law enforcement couldn't. I was not expected to succeed, of course. Rather, Angelica hoped I would get thrown overboard or something."

I told them about Spider's predilection for being dominated and how I was mistakenly assumed to be his dominatrix for the night.

"Wait," Ian's face was a confused mass of frowns. "You are saying we have a dominatrix plying her wares on board this ship?"

"Not for long," I replied. "That's not the important bit though. Attempting to do what Angelica demanded, my phone was recording as I tried to get him to talk about the murder."

Over the next few minutes, Barbie played the segment of the audio recording that was going to send Spider to jail for the rest of his life.

At the time, I'd had no clue whether he was guilty or not, though I suspected there was no smoke without fire in his particular case. Now, all doubt had been erased, for an hour after my flight from his suite, my phone recorded him ranting to Ralph about his missing bodyguard, Anton - I finally had a name for the man I knocked out – and how fearful Spider was that super sleuth Patricia Fisher knew he was guilty. He spent a full five minutes talking about how well he'd covered his tracks after the murder and how he'd then paid to make the witness vanish.

He was already in custody and in our brig but on charges that would give him a minimal jail sentence assuming his lawyers couldn't plea bargain or fend them off completely. Now we had the evidence that was needed to ensure he faced justice.

It was obvious from Ian's face that he was surprised at what my team had achieved.

"You did what no one else could," he remarked thoughtfully. "And you broke the casino case too."

Alistair cut in, "We didn't even know it was a case. All we knew was we had an accounting discrepancy. That could have gone on for weeks or months with that trio ripping us off were it not for Patricia's keen eye."

The truth was that I had stumbled across the crime completely by accident, but now was not the time to go into unnecessary detail. Not when I was so close to wrapping up and getting what I wanted.

"You came here to assess my employment, Ian. At this juncture, I feel I am within my rights to ask for a verbal opinion."

Put on the spot in a room that was entirely on my side, and therefore not on his, Ian showed why Purple Star entrusted him with such tasks.

"Very good, Mrs Fisher," he replied without looking cowed in any way. "I will say that I do not approve of your methods ..." He got shocked looks from everyone in the room, "but I cannot argue with your results. Six arrests in a single day with three crimes being solved. I would say that was a haul for anyone."

He'd given me the nod of approval, and I strode verbally forward with it.

"Thank you, Ian. I am understaffed." It was a bold statement without qualification.

Alistair looked stunned and he wasn't the only one.

"I need more people, Ian. You might be impressed by the six arrests I have made today, but I am about to send my team out to arrest a seventh."

His response was predictable. "A seventh?"

"The dominatrix," I reminded him. "Mistress Whipsnap. Her real name is Ming Na. She is staying in cabin 1204 and has been on board this ship plying her trade for two months already. I will be conducting a review of all long-term passengers to investigate any further incidences of people funding their passage through illegal activity. To that end, I need more people. Wouldn't you agree, Ian?"

He was on the spot again, and this time he squirmed.

"I'll start with Ensign Lawrie," I pointed to Molly, who reacted as if jabbed with a hot poker.

"You want me on the team?" She hadn't expected it.

The reply came not from me but from Alistair, sealing his endorsement when he said, "There's an arrest to make. Are you up for it?"

Molly was on her feet so fast I was shocked they didn't leave the deck. I had her wait until Ian promised to take my request back to headquarters and represent my proposal in a positive light.

Molly could not get her hat back onto her head fast enough. Pippin volunteered to go with her, cementing my belief that he was sweet on her. Of course, the whole team went, they had been going for two days on almost zero sleep, what with the adventure on the British Union Isles. They had a few things to wrap up, but would be in their cabins and on their own time very soon.

When they left, Molly proudly leading the way, Sam and Gloria went too. I would see Sam in the morning when there would be plenty to keep us all busy.

I saw him to the door where he surprised me with a hug.

"I was worried about you, Mrs Fisher," he admitted. "I didn't like that no one knew where you were." Now he knew how I felt when Edward Teach absconded with him and I had to wonder if he was even still alive. I didn't say that though, I hugged him back and told him to get a good night's sleep.

Ian left, satisfied that he could return to Purple Star with his task complete, and that left just five of us.

Hideki wheeled Barbie out, heading for his cabin. The two of them deserved some alone time.

Jermaine, seeing that it was just he, Alistair, and me left, bade us goodnight, and departed for his adjoining cabin.

I found Alistair's hand with mine, interlocking our fingers. I felt good about ... everything, which came as something of a surprise. It had been a hectic couple of days, and I was feeling exhausted. That was just fatigue though. Tonight, I would sleep tucked up against Alistair and with my dogs nestled into my belly.

Did I really need anything more than that?

Insomnia

Incredibly, I struggled to sleep. The plague of mysterious complaints, allegations, the suspicion over Alistair and Hennessey, and all the other drama Angelica caused me was all finished and in my rear-view mirror. However, the blissful sanctuary of slumber wouldn't co me.

There were two things troubling me.

After my friends departed, Alistair left my suite for a time. He wanted to check in on the bridge and the general running of the ship. There was always a lot going on, but it felt like that was especially true of the last few days.

Jermaine returned to run me a bath, filling it with scented oils that would leave my skin feeling soft and rejuvenated. They also made my suite smell incredible and would help me relax.

Except they didn't.

Soaking my cares away, my eyes closed and the only noise to be heard that of the water gently lapping against the sides of the bath as I breathed in and out, my phone pinged with an incoming text.

I opened one suspicious eye to glare at the infernal device. I could have ignored it, but it pinged again with another message, the sound it made taunting me. Was it work? Was it Alistair to say he'd been delayed?

Irritated because I needed to know and wouldn't relax until I did, I sat upright and peered at the screen.

Both messages were from Barbie.

She was also in the bath, but using the time to tell me what she had learned about Professor Noriega. I could have left it to the morning, but she wanted to pass the information on while it was still fresh.

Her message came with a couple of links – one to a news article. It was in Portuguese, so I couldn't read it, but I understood enough for it to confirm her claim that he was dead. The real Professor Noriega that is, not the one we met.

My blonde friend had stayed up most of the previous night, stuck in front of her laptop while Martin and the others were trying to find Jordan Jones. The research she needed to do for that task wasn't enough to keep her busy, so she had turned her attention to the coins and the professor and had made a startling discovery.

With no idea where to start her search, it was a single line on the Museum of Brazil's website that gave Barbie her first clue. They were yet to update it, so the website still showed Professor Noriega as their specialist in marine antiquities. Skim reading his bio, Barbie found his biggest passion was for one particular ship which was sent to the bottom by British warships off the coast of Columbia in 1708.

The date matched that minted onto the coins in my safe. Opening a new search, Barbie discovered all manner of conspiracy theories surrounding the ship and the suggestion that it might not have sunk at all.

That Professor Noriega – an academic man I doubted was given to flights of fantasy – believed the same, gave the theories credence.

Barbie stressed that her conclusions were just speculation, but the evidence she found was compelling enough to warrant deeper investigation. This was not least because the fake Professor Noriega had spoken about shipwrecks in our brief conversation. He brought the subject up.

Now hours later, I was lying awake in bed next to Alistair unable to get my brain to switch off. Had we stumbled across a long-lost treasure? Another link Barbie sent me was for a report on the ship and its treasure. The current estimated worth hovered around the ten-billion-dollar mark.

It was a figure I found frightening. People would kill for it. Heck, nations would go to war for less. Just a few yards from where I now lay, the safe in my suite contained a small fortune in treasure, yet potentially it was a tiny fraction of the total horde.

Had Finn Murphy found it? It would explain his murder, and why he felt it necessary to swallow the gems. I could only speculate on the circumstances of his demise, yet I was willing to bet we had the start point for a treasure hunt on our hands.

What were we going to do with it?

Before nightfall the next day, the Aurelia would dock in Rio de Janeiro. We had a two-day stopover, and one thing was for certain: we were going to the Museum of Brazil.

I closed my eyes and tried to still my brain for the umpteenth time. Thirty seconds later, they snapped open again as I acknowledged the other thing that was bothering me.

What had happened to the treacherous crew member in Angelica's employment? It was a man, and he was almost certainly part of the ship's security detachment. Beyond that, I knew nothing at all.

Cursing myself, I carefully shifted Anna and Georgie to one side and swung my legs slowly around and out of bed. I should have inter-viewed Angelica myself when she was first locked up.

Martin and Deepa had taken a statement from her, but the rest of it had been left, the team decision being that she could stew until morning when we were rested.

Ultimately, the decision meant there was a member of the crew out there who had to be fretting their secret was about to be revealed. Was Angelica in any danger?

There was an angry voice at the back of my skull telling me to go back to bed and let Angelica get what was coming to her. I was sympathetic to the voice's thoughts and opinion, but were I to wake and discover she had been killed in the night, I would never forgive myself.

Hooking a pair of shoes, and the first clothes I came to, I slipped silently from my bedroom and into the suite's living space. I would dress, quickly pop down to the brig, and return without anyone knowing I had even left the suite.

I gripped the hem of my satin negligee to pull it up and over my head. Just as I was lifting it, someone spoke, and my heart went on strike.

"Madam," said Jermaine, sitting quietly in the darkened room.

How I didn't scream I will never know, but I think I might have lost consciousness for a second as I spun around, grabbed my chest, and just about collapsed onto the carpet.

Bent over, with one hand on the edge of a couch to support myself, I held up the other hand with my index finger raised to beg a moment's grace.

Once I was sure I wasn't about to wet myself or pass out, I asked, "Sweetie, what are doing sitting in the dark by yourself?"

"Madam it occurred to me that there is still an element of the Mrs Howard-Box case that is yet to be resolved."

I managed to straighten myself up and look at him. He flicked on a table lamp.

"You're talking about the mystery crew person she had working for her?"

"Yes. If you will forgive me, madam, it is my experience that such people habitually break into your accommodation with a plan to kill you. It's that or you take it upon yourself to investigate their whereabouts in the middle of the night."

He had me bang to rights on both counts.

"I'm going down to the brig," I explained about my concerns regarding Angelica and of course he insisted on accompanying me.

I didn't argue.

Missed Clues

The ship was quiet, but not deserted. Even at close to two in the morning, there were still bars and clubs open for those who wanted to dance the night away. Those we saw were too engrossed in where they were going to pay Jermaine and me any attention and the elevator we chose to ride down to deck seven was empty the whole time.

Alighting on the lowest passenger deck, it was only a short walk to the crew elevator we needed to access the bottom six decks.

Again, the crew areas were almost, but not quite deserted.

Overhead lights blinked into life as we came near them - the passage-ways below decks unlit unless someone was in them. At the brig, the on-duty officer, Lieutenant Nutsugah, buzzed me in and appeared looking bleary-eyed with his tunic untucked and a pair of house slippers where his uniform boots ought to be.

"I wasn't expecting anyone," he admitted around a yawn which overtook his face. We had to wait for it to pass. "Who are you here to see?" he finally managed.

The brig spends most of its time empty, as it should be, and when there is a need to put someone in there, the stay is temporary. I wondered when it had last seen so many inmates.

Lieutenant Nutsugah sleepily tucked his shirt back in and swapped his slippers for his boots before waking his partners, as the brig is always manned by at least three people.

I waited, feeling a little impatient and also a little … off. I hadn't seen Angelica at any point in all of this and now I was going to be face to face with her. I wasn't sure how I was supposed to feel about it, but the dominant emotion was unhappy, winning first place over stressed by a small margin.

When the three security officers had roused Angelica and delivered her to one of the interview rooms, I sucked in a deep breath and tried my very best to banish how I felt from appearing on my face.

She was sitting behind the small white table in the centre of the room and looking at me with emotionless eyes. She said nothing as I crossed the room and took the chair opposite her. Jermaine elected to remain standing, hovering just behind my left shoulder though there was a chair free right next to me.

Angelica still hadn't spoken, so I did.

"I want to know the name of the crew person you employed, Angelica. How did you contact him? What was it that you offered for his betrayal?"

"Is that all?" she laughed. "I think I will be best served to reserve all comment until I have a legal counsel at my side."

Fighting down the rising bile I knew would come once I was in a room with her, I kept her gaze and attempted to use reason.

"Believe it or not, Angelica, I am worried for your safety."

She tipped her head back and laughed.

"Really? That's your play? You want to assume the role of the magnanimous giver, helping poor Angelica who has strayed from the path. You are a fraud, Patricia Fisher. Contacting my son was a low blow, and if I ever get the chance to come after you again, I will do so with the full might of a legal team behind me. You think this is over?" she was beginning to shout, and I held my hand up, palm out, to stop her.

"Save your breath, Angelica. I will not engage in a verbal battle with you. It comes as no surprise that you refuse to see reason – I do not remember the last time you ever did. Will you give me the name?"

She mimed zipping her mouth shut.

Pressing on, because even though my feet were twitching with the desire to leave, I needed to know I had done all I could, I said, "Whoever it is will be fretting that you will reveal their name. Either as part of a plea bargain, or simply because you see sense and start confessing, he will want to remove the possibility that his crime will be discovered. Do you hear what I am saying?"

"Yes, Patricia," Angelica replied around a bored yawn. "I hear everything you are saying. I will consider your demand if you do something for me."

"You are in no position to make bargains, Angelica," I frowned at her, barely able to believe her attitude.

"Nevertheless, I am making one. There is a man aboard this ship who has stolen from me. I want you to find Jordan Jones, Patricia. He took my money. He took all my money. He ..."

Angelica stopped speaking because I was laughing at her. My head was tipped back, and belly laughs were threatening to give me a hernia.

"You hired a hacker and he got into your bank accounts!" I managed to howl, tears running down my face. I could feel Angelica scowling at me and that just made it funnier. "You know," I spluttered, "I might just track him down so I can shake his hand!" I was barely able to control myself now and Jermaine was sniggering too.

When my mirth finally subsided a minute or more later, Angelica had reset her expression to neutral. I dearly wanted to ask if she wished to engage my services as a sleuth. I couldn't though for the laughter would start all over again before I even got the words out.

Instead, I asked, "Will you tell me the name of the crew person you employed?"

Angelica smiled and kept her lips tightly closed.

Despite still feeling highly amused, I wanted to rage at her, to raise my voice and hit her with blunt objects. To do so though would only give her ammunition. If she truly planned to fight the case against her, the only sensible thing I could do was leave.

So that is what I did.

Back in the brig's reception area while Lieutenant Nutsugah returned Angelica to her cell, I voiced my concerns to the duty officers. If one of their own came to kill Angelica, at night was when they would do it. Since she would be transferred off the ship tomorrow when we docked in Rio, any attempt to silence her would take place tonight.

I advised all three lieutenants to stay awake.

They said they would do it, but I suspected they were just telling me what I wanted to hear. Their dubious expressions told a different story.

Tired, hoping I would finally sleep now, and accepting there really wasn't anything more I could do short of electing to guard her myself, I had Lieutenant Nutsugah buzz the inner brig door open. We passed through it and closed it, as was the practice before the outer door could be opened.

The second buzzer told us the outer door's electronic lock was disabled. Jermaine pushed it open and there, right in front of us, frozen like an escaping convict in a searchlight, was Lieutenant Kashmir.

I didn't need the back of my skull to itch to know that I was looking at Angelica's inside man. Not only was there no good reason for him to be down here at this time of night, dressed as if on duty when I knew full well he wasn't, his presence brought to mind a dozen other clues I'd completely overlooked.

There was a moment when his eyes were locked on mine and no one was moving, but it lasted for no more than a fraction of a second. The spell was broken by Jermaine, who thrust himself forward to get between me and Kashmir.

Jermaine was astute enough to have arrived at the same conclusion as me and was far faster to do something about it.

Kashmir had two choices. Run or fight. On a cruise ship the guilty often run, but they never get away. Kashmir knew that and it was probably why he chose to stand his ground.

The biggest problem with that was the inconvenient fact that he was armed. I'd taken his sidearm from him hours ago, but it was gone by the time I awoke in the sickbay, so Kashmir either had it back or had been given a new one. It made little difference which it was.

He went for his gun, his right arm ripping down to grip the butt of his sidearm. I could see it beginning to clear the holster and knew Jermaine couldn't hope to get to him before he got off a shot or two. At such close range there was no chance he would miss.

A scream formed in my throat, but yet again there was too little time for it to make it past my vocal cords before Kashmir would shoot Jermaine.

Blood hammered through my head, a faraway voice telling me to, "Freeze!"

The gun went off, the sound like a cannon being fired inside my head as the close confines of the steel-lined passageway trapped all the noise and seemed to amplify it.

I was jolted by its intensity but unable to tear my eyes from the sight to my front, I saw when Jermaine was thrown to one side by the bullet.

Time stood still … wait though. I could feel the frown forming on my forehead.

Kashmir was sinking to his knees, the gun now pointing harmlessly to one side as he twitched and spasmed.

Jermaine hit the deck, but not in a heap as he might if he'd been shot, but gracefully to suggest the downward trajectory had been his choice.

Kashmir stopped twitching and pitched forward, revealing the forms of Deepa Bhukari and Martin Baker behind him. They were crouching, the pair of them still holding their taser guns.

I started breathing again, my head swimming with the sudden return of oxygen. Gasping huge breaths, I had to lean against the wall.

The lieutenants from the brig were buzzing the speaker on the entrance, shouting for someone to tell them what was going on. Their protocols barred them from leaving to investigate, but that was okay because we were going to them.

"How?" I asked Martin when I found my voice.

He pointed to his wife. "Blame her. She came up with this theory that whoever it was would need to silence Mrs Howard-Box tonight or risk having their name revealed. If they came down here in uniform, they could get into the brig, kill whoever was on duty, and kill Mrs Howard-Box."

Deepa looked up from checking Kashmir's condition and ratcheted home a set of cuffs.

"I convinced him it was worth losing some sleep to see if anyone turned up."

I could barely believe it. Just when I am done being amazed at the people I get to work with, they go and prove they are even better than I previously believed.

Jermaine was back on his feet and unruffled despite the dance with death. The bullet hadn't hit him. It hadn't even come close, burying itself in the deck when the tasers robbed Kashmir of control over his own muscles.

Lieutenant Kashmir had been a constant element in recent weeks, the reason for it apparent now. Getting closer to me during my investigations, befriending me, if you will, had all been part of his work for Angelica.

When he offered to look after my dogs, it never once occurred to me to question his motivation. His head wound, which looked nasty at the time, clearly hadn't been that bad because he'd been up and roaming the decks not so long after we found him unconscious in my cabin.

Now, I questioned whether he had ever been unconscious and cursed myself for not questioning how it was that he'd been returned so soon to active duty. No doctor would have signed off on that, not with a suspected concussion. I whacked my forehead with the palm of my right hand: he hadn't radioed for help when he chased me. It should have been the first thing he did, calling in backup and giving them my location.

He didn't want me caught though. Or rather, Angelica didn't and when he accidentally found me, he had to make it look like he was giving pursuit.

The clues had been there for me to see, but flustered, beleaguered, and in a constant state of panic as I tried to meet Angelica's demands, I had failed to separate the wood from the trees.

I stayed at the brig until Alistair arrived. Schneider and Pippin got the unenviable task of taking the news to him, but if he was mad with me for sneaking off and leaving him in bed, he was good enough not to show it.

There was work to do; another prisoner to process, and much investigation would be required to get to the bottom of the how and why of Lieutenant Kashmir's decisions.

That was not for me though. I investigate the crimes and find the evidence. What happens afterwards is someone else's problem.

It was late. Or early. I guess that depends on one's perspective. Whatever the case, I was heading back to bed. We would arrive in Rio in twelve hours, and I needed to get some sleep before we did.

That was just sensible planning on my part, for as sleep finally took me, I had no idea of the adventure that awaited me in the South American city.

Epilogue

I pushed a piece of banana through the bars of the cage, Buddy's little hand eagerly taking it from me. The Gibraltar Rock Ape continued to eye me suspiciously even though I had been visiting him daily since he got shot and had to be patched up.

"Would you like some more, Buddy?" I asked, holding up another slice of the sweet fruit.

His eyebrows wiggled for a second, his ape brain translating the sounds I was making. I offered an encouraging smile.

Buddy flipped me his middle finger.

I frowned at him through the bars of his cage.

"You are going ashore today, Buddy. I will never see you again. Can you not manage to be nice just once?"

If I needed to articulate why I felt a need to visit Buddy before he went ashore, I'm not sure I would manage to find the words. There was something about him. Something about his sense of independence and desire to be his own man ... ape.

"Well, I have to go, I'm afraid," I told him, standing up and brushing the dirt and dust from the back of my trousers. "I have a job to do."

Jordan Jones was still at large. He was the last member of Angelica's team and the master hacker who infiltrated the ship's CCTV system without anyone noticing. My floating home, the Aurelia, had docked in Rio less than half an hour ago, the task of securing the giant ship and getting it ready for the passengers to depart not even nearly done.

In anticipation that Jordan was going to try to leave, a goodly portion of the ships' security team was in plain clothes. Set to mingle with the passengers, they would search for the hacker. If he surfaced, we would catch him.

He'd taken Angelica's money; quite a large chunk of it if she was to be believed. So far as I was concerned, he'd earned it. To get it back, Angelica would have to take him to court, but I doubted she would have any luck should she try.

Other than attempting to apprehend Jordan I had no cases. That wouldn't last for long, but I hoped for at least a couple of days' respite.

It wasn't as if I had nothing to investigate.

The End

Author's Note

H ello,

Thank you for reading this book, and most especially for indulging my whimsical notes in this section. When I first started to add an author's note, it was so I could explain some of the Britishisms, or military jargon I employed when writing my Blue Moon series. I remember explaining about my father and his love for rum and how that made it into the books, and how I kept him alive in my head by recreating his character on the page.

The next book, which I will start in a day or so, is to be another Blue Moon book, the twenty first in the series, and will feature Tempest's father once again.

I wrote this Patricia Fisher story in a log cabin at the bottom of my garden in a little village in the southeast corner of England. Outside my window, the seasons shifted from winter to spring, the garden changing with it as flowers burst into life and the butterflies and bees returned.

Privileged is a word I often employ to describe myself. I get to do a thing that I love and be able to make a living from it. How many people get to say that? Better yet, I was able to discover what it was that I am good at. I work long hours very often, but the only slave driver making me do it is me because I want to tell the stories.

I was up until after midnight two nights ago, got up at five something the following morning, and then wrote until one thirty this morning in a flurry of words to get this finished. I am tired now, but my brother-in-law is coming over in a short while and we will frequent the local watering hole.

His daughter is playing with my son, the cousins close in age and firm friends. My brother-in-law needs to collect his daughter, so why not add in a visit to the alehouse that sits behind the very log cabin in which I am currently working?

It's a Friday after all.

I write about tattoos in this book. I do not have any. I may have explained this before. In the army, which was my career for many years, getting a tattoo was almost a right of passage, yet I resisted the peer pressure and I'm rather glad I did. Not that I do not admire the artistry, but the permanency worries me. Each to their own, as I have taught my children, those who enjoy being 'inked' should continue to do so.

In this book, I finally gave Patricia a gun and had her shoot someone. I managed to resist doing that for the twenty-three previous titles because it's just not what an English sleuth does. When the situation in this book demanded that she use the firearm to defend herself, I gave serious consideration to erasing the previous few thousand words so I could rewrite the scene and change it so she would have another avenue of escape. I'm glad I didn't.

Nothing about Patricia's personality or character have changed, but she has a new experience to chalk up and it came across as a fun episode for me to write within the story.

I'm going to go now, but Patricia will be back really soon.

Take care

Steve Higgs

What's next for Patricia Fisher

Rumble in Rio

When a single shot rings out to shatter the quiet at a prominent museum, it signals the start of a new mystery Patricia Fisher cannot avoid investigating.

An apparent suicide, a missing woman, a sunken treasure ship worth billions, and suspicious behaviour from almost everyone she meets ... well, that might be a lot to take for some people.

For Patricia Fisher, it's just Thursday.

She's in Rio on the trail of an altogether different mystery, however it's not long before she questions if the two cases might not be intertwined.

What did happen to Professor Noriega? Was his death a terrible accident? If so, why was there a man onboard the Aurelia pretending to be the professor?

With faithful companions at her side, our English sleuth will have to roll the dice and take some chances for she only has two days to uncover the truth.

About the Author

At school, the author was mostly disinterested in every subject except creative writing, for which, at age ten, he won his first award. However, calling it his first award suggests that there have been more, which there have not. Accolades may come but, in the meantime, he is having a ball writing mystery stories and crime thrillers and claims to have more than a hundred books forming an unruly queue in his head as they clamour to get out. He lives in the south-east corner of England with a duo of lazy sausage dogs. Surrounded by rolling hills, brooding castles, and vineyards, he doubts he will ever leave, the beer is just too goo
d.